DECEIVING THE DUKE
THE BEGUILING BARONETS
BOOK I

M. FRANCIS HASTINGS

Contents

Out in Society

Sam

Sam Acton hated every minute of escorting her sister, Sabrina Acton, to the Barrington's Ball. It was their first foray into society. Or rather, Sabrina's. For obvious reasons, Sam would never be "out" in society. Obvious reasons that crept red up the side of her neck and jaw. Some days, she could still feel the heat on her face from the flames.

Of course, it was not as visible above her cravat. And she kept her collar points rather high these days, which, fortunately, was the fashion.

For Sam Acton was now living as a man. She had been since the fire that had taken their mother and left the Acton Estate without a proper male heir.

"If you keep scowling like that, your face will freeze that way," Sabrina told her, her sister's hand pressed demurely inside Sam's arm.

"I always scowl. Freezing that way will only save me the trouble of keeping it that way myself," Sam scoffed.

Sabrina threw her blonde head back and laughed, an infectious, tinkling sound that caught the attention of every male suitor in the ballroom.

And here Sam had been worried there might not be enough candidates to choose a worthy partner for her sister.

Sabrina was technically Sam's identical twin, but the fire had taken care of that when they were just five years old. Luckily, their mother had died in childbirth so their father had made no official announcement of their birth. He'd been too heartbroken. No one but a handful of people knew Angeline Acton had given birth to twin girls.

Now, Sabrina was a shining jewel in a room full of dull baubles, and the eligible male bachelors began to swarm.

"Don't save a spot on your dance card for me," Sam murmured to her sister, forcing a smile as the men approached. It was more of a grimace, but she tried. "I want this done this week if possible so we can go back home."

"I wasn't planning to. And I'm glad you're willing to hinge my entire future on a week of courtships. It makes me feel all warm inside," Sabrina returned.

Sam pursed her lips. She supposed she was being a bit of a jerk, but she hated being away from the estate. She didn't feel safe outside it.

"Good evening, my lady. Theodore Hamilton, Lord of Kilgore." The third suitor bowed low over Sabrina's hand.

"This is the Honorable Miss Sabrina Acton." Sam introduced his sister formally again. "I am her brother, Sir Samuel Acton."

"Pleased to meet you," Theodore said, but he only had eyes for Sabrina.

Sam wanted to roll her eyes.

"Might I trouble you for two dances?" Theodore asked, making puppy-dog eyes at Sabrina.

Sabrina giggled. "Yes," she replied before Sam could stop her. "I would like that very much."

Theodore smiled and scribbled his name twice on her dance

card. As he wandered away to wait his turn, Sam leaned in and hissed in her sister's ear, "Don't do that again. We need as wide a variety as we can get."

Sabrina did roll her eyes. "Yes, master."

"Don't roll your eyes. And stop calling me 'master,'" Sam growled.

Sabrina ignored her and smiled to greet the next suitor.

Sam sighed, turned, and started because the most handsome man she'd ever seen was now standing in front of her.

"Good evening," he said. "Callum Tennant, Duke of Conford."

Sam stared at Callum until Sabrina nudged her. Then Sam cleared her throat. "Yes, of course. Forgive me, Lord Tennant. I am Sir Samuel Acton, and this is my sister, the Honorable Miss Sabrina Acton."

"Do you wish to sign my dance card?" Sabrina asked when Sam and Callum just silently regarded each other for a long moment.

Callum smiled. "Yes, of course. That is why I'm here, after all. I saw a stunning beauty across the room and could not resist. I thought I had best get my name in while there is still room!"

"A wise decision," Sam said.

"I was just marveling at how alike you look," Callum went on, looking from Sam to Sabrina, and back again.

"We're twins," Sabrina provided, and Sam wanted to smack her.

"Twins. I should have guessed." Callum scribbled his name on Sabrina's dance card then bowed over her hand. "I look forward to our dance, Miss Sabrina."

"Duke Tennant. A pleasure to meet you," Sabrina smiled.

"Likewise." Callum bowed again and disappeared into the crowd.

"Sabrina, I do not want you getting too informal with these men. One will be your husband, and he will not appreciate—" Sam scolded.

Sabrina shrugged. "You're the one who wanted me to acquire a husband as soon as possible. I have to be familiar with some of them. Otherwise, a week will not be nearly long enough."

"I could... perhaps... extend our trip to two weeks..." Sam gritted out.

"That's the brother I know and love," Sabrina beamed, kissing Sam on her good cheek.

Very soon, Sabrina's dance card was full, and Sam was able to let her go off to the dance floor, leaving time for other things. Though what other things she was supposed to be doing, she had no idea.

She gravitated toward a group of men she heard talking about politics, infiltrating the outer circle around them.

"... Are simply leeches on our society and should be driven wholesale out of London," one puffed, pompous man was saying. "The lot of them, always begging for scraps and charity. They provide no use to society."

"Then perhaps we should give them jobs," Sam piped up above the nods and murmurs of agreement.

The puffed up man blinked and peered out into the outer circle. "Who said that?" he demanded.

"I did," Sam replied with not a hint of shame.

"Are you saying it is our duty to make sure the street rats of London stop begging and go to work?" the man asked, looking around at the others who laughed.

Sam nodded. "If it is not our duty, then whose is it? We are the elite class. We provide the jobs. If we don't like having poor people in our society, we should find them work."

"And I suppose you would put them all to work on your estate, Lord..." the man sneered.

"Sir Samuel Acton," Sam said. "And I have, and I do. Because it is my societal duty. If I had work enough for all of them, I would take every one."

The man looked around again, and his cronies snickered. "Yours must be the most inefficient estate in Christendom with thieves and layabouts working there."

"They are not thieves or layabouts. Your attitude makes them so because they are desperate. What would you do to make sure your family had enough to eat, Lord...?" Sam shot back.

"*Duke* FitzRoy," he replied. "And what a silly question that is."

"So silly you cannot answer it?" Sam challenged.

The entire group fell silent.

"Wh-What?!" FitzRoy spluttered.

"He's asking if you can answer the simple question of what you would do if you hadn't inherited wealth from your father and had a family to feed." A man with a familiar voice appeared beside Sam.

Sam turned and saw Callum. "Oh. Hello."

"Hello again, Sir Samuel," Callum grinned.

"I... it... but it's a foolish question!" FitzRoy stuttered. "Duke Tennant, you cannot possibly be siding with this misguided young pup?"

"I'm simply wondering if you can answer his question. It seems you can't," Callum said. "I think, Duke FitzRoy, until you can answer it, you should be more mindful of your opinions about the poor."

FitzRoy turned bright purple. "Why, I never!"

"I'm sure you haven't." Callum winked at Sam, who just stared at him.

FitzRoy turned up his nose and stalked away, his cronies following.

"I suppose I've made an enemy there," Sam mumbled.

"Better than having made him a friend, I assure you," Callum said. "He always spouts whatever comes into his pea brain as though it is the gospel truth."

Sam chuckled. "I had a feeling."

"Now, on the other hand, I am quite interested in your views on the poor," Callum continued.

"Really?" Sam's eyebrows hit her hairline. "I'm not very popular at the local parties."

"Please. You and I both know you rarely attend even a local party," he said.

Sam blinked. "How do you know that?"

"Because I certainly would have heard of you by now," he replied.

A loud laugh escaped Sam. It was not merry and tinkling like his sister's, but a raucous, hearty guffaw. "I suppose you're right."

"I'm always right," he teased. "Now, about the poor."

Sam shrugged. "I simply believe it is our duty to ensure they have what they need. And what they need the most are jobs. Failing that, we ought to be giving them blankets and food and such. They are people, after all."

"Exactly," Callum agreed. "Finally, an educated man. You must be very well-read."

"It's a hobby," she admitted. "My favorite pastime, actually."

"Mine as well." Callum's eyes slid over to where Theodore and Sabrina were dancing. "Does your sister read?"

"Sabrina? Certainly," she replied, a strange pang in her chest as the conversation switched to Sabrina. But that was what she wanted, surely. A suitor who was interested in Sabrina, and not just for her looks. "She is not as well-read as I am. She prefers poetry and the like. But she keeps herself well-informed and has her own opinions, albeit quiet ones."

Callum nodded. "I think sometimes it's a terrible shame that women hold quiet opinions. I, for one, would like to hear what an educated woman has to say."

"I've never told Sabrina to be restrained with her words," Sam said. "It just seems that most women are more interested in embroidery, painting, decorating, and the like. I am shocked how little encouragement they receive to have opinions. But my sister is always open with me. I expect she would be with her husband as well."

"Excellent." He smiled at Sam, and it created a strange fluttering in her stomach. "I will have to quiz her during our dance. If she is half as educated and opinionated as you are, I think I might find her quite entertaining."

"I think you will," she said past a lump in her throat.

Callum watched Sabrina and Theodore for a moment longer, then turned back to Sam. "I wonder," he mused. "What are your opinions on slavery?"

"I believe it to be a reprehensible practice. A person cannot be owned," Sam spat.

"You are a Whig through and through," Callum laughed.

Sam eyed Callum. "And you?"

"Just as much a Whig as you are," Callum admitted. "I believe slavery to be an antiquated, unnecessary, immoral practice that should have left with the rebel brutes who decided to instigate it in the colonies."

"Thirteen colonies in particular," Sam grunted. "It amazes me they are so forward in their government yet so backward in their practices. One can hardly blame them for rising up and breaking away from the Empire, however, it disappoints me that they have continued the practice of slavery even while declaring they are a land of freedom."

Callum's lips twitched. "And your thoughts on a woman's right to vote?"

"Please. Of course women should vote. And a lot of these old wills excluding women from holding land ought to be burned," Sam responded passionately.

"I suppose you come from such an estate," he said.

"I do," she replied. "And thank God almighty my mother had a male heir else we'd be in real trouble. Living in a rookery or Lord only knows where." A knot formed in Sam's stomach. She felt bad for lying to this man for some reason.

"My lands have a similar clause attached. As you say, it is good my mother had a male heir. She died in childbirth, and my father would never have taken another wife," Callum confessed. "And your mother? Does she yet live? I assume your father does not as he is not escorting your sister among the ton."

Sam rubbed the scarring along her jaw. "Our mother also died in childbirth. My stepmother in a fire when we were quite young."

Callum's eyes widened. "My apologies for bringing up such a painful memory. It is good you survived."

"Yes, thank you," Sam said half-heartedly. She didn't always believe it had been for the best herself. But then, for Sabrina's sake, it was good she had survived.

For Sabrina's sake, Sam could do just about anything.

I Could Have Danced All Night

Sabrina

The men passed in a blur of dances. Sabrina could hardly keep up. She danced fine, but names escaped her, and one terrible time, she called a suitor by the wrong name.

He was gracious about it, but Sabrina still felt awful.

How was she supposed to choose in a week? They were all so handsome and eligible and held this land and connections. Sam would surely be looking for land and connections. Sabrina really wished there was time for someone to stir her heart.

She was on the edge of numbness in her mind and her feet from all the talking and whirling around when Lord Theodore Hamilton came for his first turn. Sabrina blinked tiredly at him.

Theodore laughed and took her hand, tucking it into his arm. "Why don't we adjourn this first dance to the punch table? It's hard work being out on the floor all the time."

Sabrina sagged with gratitude. "My Lord, you have no idea how pleased I am to hear you say that. Please forgive me for costing you this dance."

He grinned. "Come, let us find you a chair. Then we can talk properly."

Theo hunted about and finally kicked a young lordling out of a chair so Sabrina could sit down. She apologized profusely, but the lordling simply smiled, bowed, and said, "It's a privilege."

A look from Theo as he reclined against the wall had him scampering off. He sipped some of his punch. "I suppose if we are to have what is considered a proper conversation, I'll be forced to remark that it is quite hot in here."

Sabrina looked up. "I suppose you might."

"Then you must say something about how too many couples were invited," he teased.

A flutter started in her chest, and she smiled. "I suppose I should. And then, by and by, you must comment on today's weather."

"And the state of the roads," he agreed solemnly.

"Yes, of course, we cannot ignore the state of the roads," she replied.

He smiled. "Or perhaps we could start off on a different foot. Your name is Miss Sabrina Acton. Your brother is Sir Samuel Acton. Are there more members of your family?"

She winced. "I'm afraid not. My mother died in childbirth, my stepmother in a fire many years ago, and my father died of pining for her. My stepmother and my father were a true love match, you see."

"And you hope for the same," Theo inferred.

With a blush, she nodded. "I do."

"Then we have something in common already." His smile could have lit the whole room.

The fluttering feeling started again in her chest. "It is good to find common interests," she noted.

"Yes. That's a good start." Theo glanced out at the crowd and chuckled. "Your brother is not a very good chaperone. He's gotten into a debate with Duke Callum Tennant. Now I'll never hear the end of my friend's politics this evening."

Sabrina looked over at her brother and saw that, indeed, he was not paying any attention to her. "Perhaps I should frighten him and go out on the veranda with you."

Theo's eyebrow shot up. "Miss Sabrina, that would be quite improper without a chaperone. It would besmirch your honor, and I would have no choice but to marry you."

"I suppose we shall keep it in mind for the next ball, then," she teased.

He let out a bark of laughter, making several people turn. But not Sam or Callum. "My, oh my, I will have my hands full, it seems. I don't suppose you also talk about politics?"

"Most women find it unseemly," she said evasively.

Theo looked down at her, and his eyes twinkled. "But I'm sure a brother who can absorb Tennant so, having no one else on his estate to debate with, will have encouraged his sister to form her own opinions."

"My opinions, as you might imagine, very much mirror my brother's, so there is little debate, but much discussion," Sabrina admitted.

"Your brother would not begrudge you your own opinion, though," Theo said.

"Never. He encourages me to have my own thoughts," she replied. "It's just that he's very well-read and educated on the politics of the day, and when he tells me what the various debates are, I can only be amazed there is another side sometimes. He has very strong opinions on our responsibility to help the poor, for instance, and I cannot disagree. I am quite proud that my brother does not just spout his opinions, but also puts his beliefs into practice. We employ several people from the area who might otherwise have ended up in a rookery."

Theo nodded slowly. "I'm glad you believe so because Duke FitzRoy continually tells me how I shall be cheated out of my fortune by the poor I employ. Tennant also employs those who would have otherwise been destitute."

"Duke FitzRoy sounds heartless," she said, then put a hand to her mouth. "I did not mean to insult a high-ranking member of the ton on my first day out in society."

"Have no fear. I won't tell a soul." He grinned. "But, privately, I agree with you."

She giggled. "I'm glad I will not be stricken from every guest list in London just today."

"The night is young," he said.

Sabrina's giggle turned into a tinkling laugh. "I suppose it is."

"Have you rested enough? I believe they are playing our song." He smiled, and she listened as a waltz began.

"This was all part of your nefarious plan to get your dance to be a waltz," she accused him lightly.

"Ah, foiled again. Or am I?" he asked, holding out his hand.

Sabrina rose and put her glass on the tray of a passing servant. "Why not?"

Theo escorted Sabrina out onto the dance floor, and they performed an enchanting waltz. When the music ended, she gave a deep sigh of regret that had to take the next man on her dance card.

"Just remember," Theo reminded her. "I have two dances on that card."

Her smile returned. "I shall hold you to it."

❧

ANOTHER NUMBER OF UNMEMORABLE MEN TWIRLED HER around the floor. But the damage was done. Sabrina only had eyes for Theo.

For his part, Theo did not dance with any other woman that night, waiting patiently instead for his second turn with Sabrina.

She was flattered, and when he did finally come around again, she nearly ran from the man she'd been dancing with to join Theo's company.

"Do you need another rest?" he asked.

"I've been waiting to dance with you all night. If you asked it of me, I could fly," she said giddily before she could stop the words from coming out of her mouth.

His gaze softened. "Perhaps at the next ball we shall both fly and see what the others have to say."

"I care less and less what others think, I find, as the night wears on." She sighed, color high in her cheeks.

As they passed each other during the group dance, Theo whispered, "I would beg a third dance, but that would certainly ruin your reputation. At least, until we are properly engaged."

Sabrina's pulse picked up. "Will you call on me, then? Please arrange it with my brother. I would like to see you."

"A thousand men could not stop me," he assured her.

She continued the cotillion with him, pleased to her toes Theo would come to call.

When the song ended, Sabrina prepared herself to dance with the next man on her card only to have Theo offer her his arm again.

"You look parched, my dear," he said with a grin.

"Why thank you, Lord Hamilton. I must say I am," she replied politely, trying to suppress a laugh and failing miserably.

As they walked back over to the punch bowl, he said in a low tone, "Say it again."

"Say what?" she asked.

"My name."

Sabrina's heart melted. "Lord Hamilton," she breathed.

"Miss Acton," he responded, and she felt as though she was floating. "I dare not say more until I have met with your brother, but I am most pleased I did not skip the Barrington's Ball tonight."

"I am most pleased you are here as well," she said softly. "Now, what shall we talk about if not the roads?"

Theo graciously took the lighthearted turn in conversation. "I don't suppose you have read Lord Byron?"

"Oh, he is one of my favorites!" she exclaimed.

"'She walks in beauty, like the night,'" he quoted to her. "It makes me think of you."

A flush grew on her cheeks. "Thank you. That is a beautiful verse to be compared to."

"Which is your favorite?" he asked.

"Of Lord Byron's or of all poetry?"

"Excellent question. I think I would like to hear your most favorite of all poetry," he said.

"'Love sought, is good; but given unsought, is better,'" she responded.

His eyes lit up. "Shakespeare."

"I've always thought there was truth in that. It is a short line from *Twelfth Night*, but I think it is the truest line he ever wrote," Sabrina explained.

"Then let us toast to love given unsought," he said, tapping his punch glass to hers.

She smiled so brightly she swore it should make her face hurt. But she was so happy that she didn't feel a thing. "To love given unsought."

"I will call on you," Theo murmured. "Though I am sure I will need to impress your brother if I am to..."

"If you are to?" she prodded.

"Ah, but I forget myself. A man could forget himself forever in your blue eyes." He sighed. "There are words a gentleman must not say too prematurely. I would hate to break your heart later."

Sabrina's heart thudded in her chest. "Lord Hamilton, if my brother does not settle on you, it will break my heart. I know it must be too soon to say such things, but my brother never encouraged me to be anything but forthright."

"I like that about you," he whispered.

"Then we haven't any problems." Sabrina emptied her glass and set it aside . "Come, let us go see my brother before he wonders if you've stolen me."

Theo looked around and grinned. "Your brother is far too wrapped up in speaking to Tennant to worry if I've stolen you."

Sabrina gazed in her sister's direction, and, sure enough, she was still talking to Callum—passionately if her sharp, wide gestures were anything to go by. But Callum glanced at Sabrina from time to time, making her feel as though she had a new chaperone. "I believe your friend Duke Tennant has taken my brother's place."

"Someone should have. You never know what nefarious ideas I have rattling around my head," he teased.

She smiled and nodded in her sister's direction. "Perhaps we should join them before Duke Tennant comes storming over to demand his dance."

"Ah, yes, he did claim a dance with you, didn't he?" Theo said.

"The last one of the evening," she confirmed. "I could pretend to have twisted my ankle?"

"No." He shook his head. "Tennant is a good man. It would be petty of me to ask you to fake a sore ankle in order to quell my jealousy."

"So you will be jealous?" Sabrina grinned.

Theo offered her his arm again. "Insanely."

"Good." She took his arm, and they walked around the perimeter of the ballroom together, heading toward Callum and Sam.

"Tennant was right, though," Theo said as they approached the others.

"Oh? How so?" Sabrina asked.

"Your brother and you look very much alike." He regarded Sam as they approached. "Even for twins."

Sabrina felt bad lying to Theo, but it wasn't as though she could tell him the truth. Then their cousin Jeremy would strip Acton from them, and they would be little better than beggars. "Many people say that."

"Is the scarring from the fire that took your mother?" Theo asked quietly so Sam wouldn't hear.

"My stepmother, but yes," Sabrina replied simply. "Sam was most unfortunate to be caught in the blaze."

"A pity. It must cast a pall over his ability to secure a good marriage," Theo replied.

It took everything in Sabrina not to wince. "You have no idea," she muttered.

In Want of a Wife

Callum

It appeared that Miss Sabrina Action and Theo were very taken with each other when Callum watched them on the dance floor. This was a bit of a problem as, watching Sabrina interact with others with a natural grace and ease, he was also a bit taken with the woman. He could tell already she would make some man an excellent wife, and was thinking that man might as well be him.

Callum wasn't really looking for a love match, just a wife who would be a great hostess at parties, not bad-looking, and with enough of her own interests that she wouldn't be underfoot all the time. That Miss Sabrina Acton might actually have thoughts and opinions of her own beyond embroidery and music was an unexpected bonus.

But he would have to speak with her first to ascertain if what Sam said was true. Sam himself was delightful and would make a most excellent brother-in-law. Callum could already imagine the fierce debates they would have on intellectual topics of all kinds. If only they didn't agree on so many things.

"Miss Acton, how lovely for you to join us." Callum smiled as

Theo escorted Sabrina to the group while Sam was mid-sentence, speaking on the state of trade between England and other nations.

Sam stopped and blinked as though noticing Sabrina for the first time. "Yes, I am most pleased to see you both," he said, recovering.

Callum had to smile again. Sam was positively endearing. Young and full of fire. "Don't worry, Acton. I've been keeping a weather eye on your sister for some time now."

His cheeks flushed while Theo, Sabrina, and Callum shared a good laugh. "I have been a most inattentive brother. I apologize, Sabrina."

"It's all right," she replied. "As His Grace says, he has been most attentive in your stead."

"Hmm." Theo gave Callum a look of challenge.

He gave him the same look back. The game was on. "It is not difficult to be attentive to one as elegant as yourself, Miss Acton," Callum said.

Callum supposed he would have to broker with Sam directly if he decided he liked Sabrina enough to oust Theo. Theo might be a lord, but Callum was a duke. He would be superior marriage material in any brother's eyes.

She did not let go of Theo's arm until Sam looked pointedly at her. Callum suppressed a grin. Brother dear was not as sold on Theo yet as his sister was.

"Lord Hamilton was just saying he might like to come to call on me," Sabrina said, reluctantly taking her hand off of Theo's arm.

"Lord Hamilton is welcome to call," Sam responded, though his narrowed eyes told Theo to behave himself.

Her smile was like sunshine and Callum knew in that moment he would fight Theo for her. Any woman who could light up a room like that was worthy of being his wife. "I would also like to call, Acton, if you would allow it." He tested the waters with the use of just Sam's surname.

Sam's smile was almost as brilliant. Callum had made a fast friend in him. That would do nothing but increase his chances.

However, if Sam did settle on Theo, Callum would still like to stay in touch. An intellect paired with a passion like his was a rare find in the peerage. "You would also be most welcome, Hamilton."

"You have not danced with any of the ladies here, Acton," Theo interrupted, trying to inveigle himself into his good graces. "Your sister has led me to believe you are unmarried. Are you not going to try your hand?"

Callum's heart squeezed as Sam touched the burn scar just visible above his collar points. If one looked closely enough, one could see the burn went all the way down his neck, disappearing under his shirt. It must then travel lower still. Callum wanted to slap Theo for being so crass and shot him a glare.

For his part, Theo had already recognized his mistake, as Sabrina was also glowering at him. "I didn't mean to imply... that is to say, Acton, you are perfectly good-looking. There is no reason..."

"Why don't you stop while you're behind," Callum said.

"I think I shall," Theo sighed. "I am sorry. No insult was meant."

"I intend to leave the estate of Acton to one of my sister's sons. Perhaps the second or third. It depends on who is inheriting the least," Sam explained. "I am not in the market for a wife, as they say."

"That is indeed a pit—" Theo began.

Callum decided to save the idiot. "I was most impressed that Acton stood up to Duke FitzRoy on the subject of the poor."

Theo blinked. "He did what?"

"My brother has very strong opinions about our responsibilities to the poor," Sabrina said. "It would not surprise me in the least if he stood up to the king himself on the subject."

"I thought as much." Callum grinned at Sam.

He gave me a relieved smile back.

"Well, that was uncommonly stupid," Theo gaped.

Sam's eyebrows drew together in both affront and confusion. Callum knew he was a shoe-in now to be Sabrina's husband. Calling your potential wife's brother stupid was not exactly the best way to curry his favor. "Pardon?"

"Duke FitzRoy is very well-respected, or might I say feared, in society. I doubt you will receive many invitations to social events after this if you have angered him," Theo said.

Confusion turned to worry and Sam looked to Callum.

"He has a point," he confirmed. "But I still think it was rather noble."

Sam groaned and put a hand to his forehead. "The whole point of this trip is to find Sabrina a suitable husband. If we are not invited to any events, that is going to be quite difficult."

"I think you may have impressed more men than you think. You haven't ruined her chances with me," Callum said.

"Nor me," Theo piped up.

Sam glanced from Callum, to Theo, and back again. "To be honest, gentlemen, I was hoping Sabrina would have more than her pick of the lot."

"A duke and a lord are not sufficient contenders for her hand?" Callum teased. It warmed his heart when Sam blushed. He was so fun to tease.

"Yes, well, that is all very well and good, of course," he stuttered.

Sabrina sighed. "I'm right here."

"Yes, generally the discussion of marriage would happen in your office, not in the ballroom with Miss Acton standing right here," Callum said.

Sam blew out a long breath. "I am but a country baronet, and my father brokered no marriages to be an example to me, so I apologize if I am trouncing upon decorum. However, as it is her future, I would like Sabrina to be intimately involved in the process. When you say such discussions would happen in my office, Sabrina would be there anyway, unless she and I had come to an agreement beforehand."

Sabrina raised her chin defiantly at Callum. He couldn't help but enjoy that trait as well. It reminded him of her brother.

"I believe it may be too early to speak of marriage to either one of you," he went on, his brow furrowed in the most adorable manner as he thought about it. "I'd like Sabrina to have the opportunity to get to know you better, that much I do know."

"It is only fitting, of course," Callum replied.

"That sounds like an excellent idea," Theo added.

"Therefore," Sam decided. "You shall both come to call at our London house and I will act as chaperone as you spend time with my sister. But do know you will likely not be the only two in the running."

Callum winced. "After what happened with Duke FitzRoy, Acton, I must tell you that we might be."

He closed his eyes and sighed. "Then I must tell you I am sorry, Sabrina, and if there are no others, I hope you and I can settle on one of these two."

"That shouldn't be an issue," she responded, smiling at Theo.

Indeed, Callum was starting out behind. No matter. He was sure he'd catch up. He knew he could be just as charming as Don Juan there.

The quartet struck up the music for the last dance, and Callum smiled at Sabrina. "Shall we? I believe I am last on your dance card."

She frowned ever so briefly before her charming expression was fixed into place. "I would love to dance with you," she lied easily.

Callum wanted to laugh, but also put on his most charming self and offered her his arm.

Sabrina took it and walked with him out onto the dance floor.

"You're quite taken with Hamilton," Callum observed without preamble as they began to dance a cotillion. He wanted to see if she would rise to the bait.

"I like him. I suppose it is more fitting to hide my regard, but he regards me as well, so I don't see the point of a charade," she replied.

Polite, yet opinionated. Much like her brother. Though Sam might be a bit less polite. It was an endearing trait in both of them, regardless. "I hope you will not be offended if I court you as well."

"Why should I be offended? I would be quite flattered, though, I will tell you, as things stand, your chances of my support are slim," she confessed.

"I like a challenge," Callum said. "I think you will find, in time, I am every bit as charming as Hamilton, if not more so."

She inclined her head, giving me a long look. "I think you are more enamored of my brother than you are of me."

"Is that so wrong? A man should get along with his brother-in-law," Callum laughed. "Besides, I've had little chance to get to know you, nor you me."

"True," she conceded the point. "Though if you are looking for a misbehaving wife who will alienate the whole of the ton, you are looking in the wrong direction. I am a refined young lady."

"Of that I have no doubt. But I do like a woman with her own opinions," Callum said.

Sabrina smiled at that. "That is a very attractive quality in a man, I must say."

"Ah, then I am not so far back in the running." he winked.

She regarded me thoughtfully. "We'll see."

To her credit, she did not take her attention off him the entire dance, though Callum could feel Theo staring daggers at his back. When the dance was finished, he brought her back to their little group.

Theo was red in his cheeks, while Sam had a look of displeasure on his face.

"What did I miss?" Callum asked.

"I was trying to explain myself," Theo replied. "That the scarring—"

"Lord Hamilton, you must let that go," Sabrina cut him off, giving her brother a sympathetic glance.

Callum grimaced and gently deposited her next to her brother. "I will take care of this." He gripped Theo's arm and dragged him several yards away.

"Are you trying to lose?" he asked him.

"No, I... I was just trying to point out to Acton that he shouldn't be so self-conscious about his scars and should try his hand with the ladies," he said.

"Hamilton. The scarring extends past his collar, perhaps a good deal lower." Callum gave him a significant look.

It took him a moment, but then Theo's jaw dropped. "You think he's not whole?"

"I think it's a possibility. At any rate, it's obviously an embarrassment to him and you need to stop. Acton is a good man, and a good brother. His own personal struggles are his own." Loyalty flared in Callum's chest for the young man. He didn't deserve to be the subject of gossip, which no doubt he would be, both for his scarring and for defying Duke FitzRoy.

"You're right." Theo nodded. "I was being insensitive. And I'm sure it's hurt my chances."

"All the better for me." Callum grinned at him.

Jeremy Acton

Sam

Sam stood with Sabrina, watching Callum give Theo a dressing down. She had to admit, Callum was a fascinating man, and for just a moment, she'd been jealous when his regard turned to her sister. But only for a moment. That he liked her sister was for the best, and if Sam was very lucky, perhaps Callum would be her brother-in-law. She thought of the fierce debates they might have in the future. If only they didn't agree on so much.

"Sam, there you are," She heard a familiar, dreaded voice from a few yards away.

"Is that...?" Sabrina whispered.

"It's cousin Jeremy," Sam confirmed, plastering a smile on her face, as did her sister, and they turned to face the man that threatened their very existence.

"Wonderful ball, wouldn't you say?" Jeremy asked as he joined them. "Sabrina, you are looking lovely as always."

She gave a slight curtsy. "Thank you, Jeremy. Yes, it is a lovely ball."

"Sam, keeping my estate in order, I trust?" He winked at Sam. "What brings you to town? I'd always thought you were too ashamed to leave the estate."

Her sister gasped. "Jeremy! That is extremely impolite!"

"It's extremely true." He gave Sam a longer look than she was comfortable with then grinned. "You know, everyone is wondering if those scars go *all* the way down, if you catch my meaning."

"Don't be vulgar," Sam snapped. "It matters little either way, don't you think? The estate will be going to one of Sabrina's sons."

Jeremy's smile faltered. "You would forget about your city cousin?"

"You only started showing up after our father died," Sam continued while Sabrina held onto her arm and raised her chin proudly. "And that was never to help us after. You just came to assess what you thought would be your estate. But it won't be, Jeremy. Not now, not ever. So you can keep your jokes, and every ounce of rudeness and vulgarity in them, to yourself. That we are family aggrieves me every day."

"I feel the same way," Jeremy said sweetly. "Pity you didn't die in that fire. Then I would be the one finding Sabrina a good match, and Acton would be mine."

"A greater pity that would be. I'm sure you'd be whipping our workers even as we speak," she hissed.

Jeremy snorted. "You've always had such strange views about the poor—which you managed to share with Duke FitzRoy, I hear." He chortled. "Sabrina is never getting married. You've managed to ruin her chances in one night. Not that I'm surprised."

"Actually," a voice behind me said.

Sam jumped and turned. There were Callum and Theo, looking distinctly displeased with Jeremy.

"We're both vying for Miss Acton's hand," Callum finished, putting a hand on her shoulder.

Theo offered Sabrina his arm, and she took it. "I think Miss

Acton and I will take a turn about the room. This is not the sort of conversation that is appropriate for nice young ladies."

"Yes, do," Callum and Sam agreed together.

With a sneer at Jeremy, Theo took her away.

"Ah, now we can be blunt," Jeremy said.

"What were we being before?" Sam asked.

"Tactful." Jeremy raked his eyes over him, stopping at his crotch. "Do you have a twig and berries or not?"

Her jaw dropped. True, she hadn't been raised a lady, but some things affronted the senses regardless.

"That is exceedingly vulgar," Callum growled. "Are you drunk?"

He gave a half-shrug. "Does that really matter?"

"I don't know. I suppose I couldn't think less of you at this point, drunkard or not," Callum said.

"It is you who came barging in on a private conversation," Jeremy pointed out.

"The subject of which is unseemly even for a young man." Callum squeezed Sam's shoulder and then let his hand drop. "Why don't you try that kind of vulgarity at a gentlemen's club. See where it gets you."

"Are you challenging me to fisticuffs?" he chuckled nastily.

Callum glared at him. "One of us should have challenged you to a duel by now."

A duel? Sam didn't like the idea of Callum getting shot on her account. "Gentlemen, please. Let us just leave it at that. Jeremy said something tasteless. He's been properly chastised." She glared at him. "I hope."

"I still want to know the answer," Jeremy said.

She'd had it. Her hand balled into a fist at her side.

"Let us take this out to the gardens," Callum interjected quickly, moving to stand between Jeremy and Sam. "We don't want to scandalize the entirety of society, now do we?"

"What would it matter? Sam already did," he snarked.

"Are you saying you're afraid to fight me?" Sam asked, pushing up her sleeves. A nasty burn scar ran the length of her left forearm.

"I'm saying I don't fight invalids," Jeremy sniffed. He turned away.

Callum grabbed his arm. "We're going out to the gardens. A gentleman of honor has challenged you. I suppose you won't answer the challenge, being that you have no honor?"

He rolled his eyes. "Fine. I'll beat the little brat cripple to a pulp."

"We'll see," she muttered. She spun on her heel and headed out to the veranda, then into the gardens themselves.

The two men walked behind her.

Sam found a nice little secluded area between the hedges and squared up on Jeremy, holding her fists up. She was raised a boy, after all, and her father had thought part of that education would necessarily be how to fight as she was always going to be smaller than most other men.

Her cousin laughed again, but this time with a bit of nerves. "You have a good fighting form," he commented.

"Someone my size needs to be good at some things more than others. I detest fighting, but someone needs to teach you a lesson in manners," Sam gritted out.

He held up his hands. "Let us say I've learned my lesson, then. I have no desire to hurt you. Quite obviously, you've suffered enough."

"Are you saying you don't think you can beat him?" Callum asked.

"If you get in one punch, Jeremy, I will be very much surprised," Sam said.

Jeremy gave a hard swallow. "I was not educated in fisticuffs," he finally admitted.

"If you prefer pistols at dawn..." Callum suggested.

Sam shook her head. "I have no desire to shoot my cousin."

"Who said you'd be doing the shooting? He offended my sensibilities as well," Callum said.

Jeremy turned very pale indeed. "I would prefer to make this unseemly incident simply go away."

"Coward," Callum grunted.

Sam patted Callum on the back. "Don't bother baiting him. You are above his level." She turned to Jeremy. "I would appreciate it if you forgot we were cousins and did not approach Sabrina or me while we are in London. Our business will be concluded presently, and we will darken your city no longer."

"That I can do, believe me," he agreed. He then quickly stalked away from them.

"You do have a very good fighting form," Callum observed when Jeremy was gone.

She shrugged. "It's true what I said. Since I am a smaller man, it is important that I am still able to defend my sister and myself. I don't want people thinking they can do nefarious things to us just because I wouldn't be able to fight back."

"I'm sure you would earn a fearsome reputation in the underground fighting rings," he told her. "I'd bet on you, at least."

Sam smiled at him. "Thank you. That means more than you think."

"Enough to consent to giving me your sister's hand?" he asked.

Her smile faded.

"I'm joking," he grinned.

She laughed a little bit but was more caught off guard by the wave of jealousy that washed over her when he mentioned marrying her sister. Of course, he would want to marry her sister. That was the whole point of this blasted trip—to get Sabrina properly married off.

Callum gave me a curious look but then shrugged. "We should go back inside. Your sister is without a proper chaperone."

"That is true," Sam replied. "You don't have any worries about Hamilton, do you?"

"None at all," he chuckled. "But it is always best to do what's proper."

"I have a feeling I'm going to learn that lesson the hard way in society," she sighed. They started to walk back to the ballroom.

"Yes," he agreed. "But I rather like that about you."

Sam snorted. "That I'm a social illiterate? I have no idea who not to offend in society. No idea who to ingratiate myself with."

"That you're passionate enough not to stand for social graces that get in the way of what's right," he said.

She blinked at him. "Oh. That sounds rather nice when you put it that way."

"It's a rather nice quality to have." They stopped in the same place in the sweltering ballroom that they had been standing in before.

"What I ought to do is take Sabrina back to the London house before she gets the vapors," Sam muttered, resisting the urge to fan herself. She envied Sabrina her fan, but then, she was wearing far more layers than she was, so if one of them deserved a fan, it was her.

"Not a bad notion." He waved to Theo who began making his way back with Sabrina.

Sam saw Jeremy was in their path, but as he'd promised, he moved out of the way without a word. But something else had changed since Callum and Sam had been gone. There were a lot of fans over mouths. Collective whispering reigned while many stole furtive glances at her.

"I have a very bad feeling," she said to him as they waited for Sabrina's and Theo's return.

Callum darted his gaze around, frowning. "I do as well."

A giggling girl who was barely old enough to be out in society grabbed Theo's arm as Sabrina and he passed. She leaned up and whispered something in his ear.

Theo's eyes widened and he shook her off, starting to give her a good telling off before Sabrina stopped him.

Sam had a sinking suspicion she knew what the topic of conversation among the ton had become.

Sabrina tugged Theo toward them, and he reluctantly followed.

"Let me guess," Sam said when they were close enough to keep his voice low. "The topic of gossip has now turned to twigs and berries?"

Theo sighed and nodded. "I'm sorry. I don't know who started the rumor."

"I do." Sam's jaw clenched, and she glared at Jeremy who just smiled back at her with the most infuriating grin.

"Who?" Theo asked.

"Our cousin, no doubt," Sabrina said angrily.

"Jeremy Acton," Callum supplied when Theo looked confused.

"That ass?" Theo replied. Then he winced. "I apologize, Miss Acton. I was just taken by surprise."

"You're not wrong," she said.

Sam waved a hand tiredly. "I'd have been shocked as well to find that he was family to either one of you. Unfortunately, one cannot choose one's family."

"Why would he spread such terrible rumors about his own family?" Theo asked.

"Because he's an ass." Sam shook his head. "No, it's more than that. He was hoping to inherit the Acton Estate, but then my mother had a boy. He's bitter."

"I would birth a hundred babies just to ensure that man never got his hands on Acton," Sabrina declared.

"A hundred?!" Callum and Theo protested together.

She blushed. "All right. Maybe not a hundred. But a great many."

"It would be a great service to the Crown to keep that man from getting his hands on your estate, I'm sure," Callum said.

"I have no fear of him getting it. Sabrina will have at least one boy, and that, as they say, will be that," Sam responded.

Theo and Callum nodded, though Theo did give her a strange look.

Sam sighed. "Because we are among friends, no, I will not be having any children. Whether I can or cannot is still up for debate."

Callum raised an eyebrow at Theo, who looked suitably ashamed of his curiosity.

"I think it would be best if Sabrina and I left now. Do enjoy your evening," Sam said to both of them. "And please, call at Eleven Charles Place at any time."

"We will," they responded together.

About the Twins

Theo

As he watched them go, Theo couldn't help but keep his eyes on Sabrina. She was so sweet and beautiful, inside and out. And she was opinionated, which just made her even sweeter in his estimation.

"You want her for a wife." He'd almost forgotten Callum was there.

Theo turned back to him. "I do."

"I do as well. How ever will we settle this?" he grinned.

He was sure Callum was about to come up with a wager of some sort, but for once, he was uninterested. "I think we should just let her choose."

His eyebrows shot up. "That's surprisingly unlike you, Hamilton. I thought you were always interested in a good bet."

"Not this time. This time, there is too much on the line," he said.

He inclined his head at me. "Well, well. I guess our young lord has grown up."

"I'm the same age as you," Theo reminded him.

"True. But you always lacked my maturity," he teased.

"Thank you." He looked around at the others still conversing and had the most overwhelming sense of boredom. Without Sabrina there, everything seemed very dull.

"I was just thinking. Maybe we should go to the club. All the evening's entertainment seems to have left," Callum echoed his thoughts.

Theo laughed. "You won't get me drunk enough to wager with you."

He held up his hands. "I wouldn't dream of trying."

"Liar. But yes, let's adjourn to another environment. It is quite stuffy in here, the quality of the company has gone down considerably, and you or I may punch one of the gossips," Theo suggested.

"Especially Jeremy Acton. Deserving though he is, it would be a shame to be banned from society events for the rest of the season," he said. "How would we scandalize the ton by showing up with Acton and his sister?" He started toward the doors, and Theo followed beside him.

"You are quite impressed with Acton," Theo observed.

Callum shrugged. "He's a riveting discussion partner. If you hadn't found every way to insult him, you might have found that out for yourself."

"I doubt you would lose Acton if you backed out and let me have Miss Acton," he tried.

He grinned. "Nice try. True, I would still have Acton for a friend, but he is settled in his country life. I doubt I would see much of him without an excuse to visit or for him to visit me. I believe that would be a terrible shame. And his sister is versed in politics and has her own opinions, according to him, so I believe that would be a good foundation for wedded bliss. At least she would be a proper mother to our children, not one of those insipid young things who fawn over lace and such as though it were a profession."

"I think I love her, Tennant," Theo finally confessed.

"Hmm. You've known her for the span of an evening. That cannot be quite long enough to determine that," he scoffed.

"I think it was long enough," he argued.

Callum laughed. "Hamilton, you are a hopeless romantic."

"And you are hopelessly jaded," he countered.

"True. But that doesn't mean I'm going to give up on a quality wife," he said. "I do have to settle down at some point. Heirs do not pop out of the brush."

"You just wish there were women out there who were more like men. Perhaps like Acton?" Theo accused.

Callum sorted. "There are no women like Acton. No woman would match wits with me, even if she could. They are all taught to be demure, empty-headed fools as though that is what men are looking for. Miss Acton being a rare exception."

"There are few men who are looking for more than that," he pointed out. "They are just pandering to the largest population of men, which is shrewd, if you think about it."

"I suppose. It makes things deucedly dull for the rest of us, however." He looked up at the night sky as we walked deeper into town. "Then again, they have to suppress their intellects because there are also few men of any quality in society. It was hard enough finding a friend in you."

"And I am not nearly as politically-minded as your new friend Acton," he chuckled.

"That does not make you any less my oldest and truest friend," he said.

Theo smiled at him. "Would my oldest and truest friend let me have Miss Acton?"

"Your oldest and truest friend would consider it if you could find me a woman of equal quality," he replied.

"That's impossible!" Theo protested.

"Exactly my point."

"Well, I suppose we shall just agree to let the best man win on this one. And stay friends after, of course." The last part was particularly important to Theo. Callum had been his friend almost all his life, and he didn't want this to come between them either way.

Callum looked over at him with a serious expression on his face.

"Of course we shall remain friends after, whichever way Acton decides."

"Ah yes. You woo the brother while I woo the lady herself. That her brother has the final word does make my task more difficult," he admitted.

"You did it to yourself. What possessed you to ask about his scarring?" he asked.

"Clearly some rogue imp was whispering in my ear tonight because I have no idea," Theo sighed. "I really was trying to bolster his confidence. He is not a bad-looking sort, scars or no."

Callum nodded at that. "He looks almost disturbingly like his sister, if you take in his appearance for a while. I had no idea a girl and a boy twin could look so alike."

"Perhaps you should give up on the sister and bugger the brother instead," he chuckled.

He punched Theo in the shoulder. "Don't be crass."

"Defending the young man's honor as well? You've got it bad," he continued to tease.

Callum rolled his eyes. "Fine. Think what you like. It's not going to stop me from courting his sister."

"And we have come full circle."

"Indeed we have. And we have come to the club as well." He gestured for Theo to enter before him.

Cigar and cigarillo smoke wafted out of the doorway as the two men stepped inside. They went immediately to the card tables and began to gamble.

That night, Theo won and fleeced Callum for a fair bit of money, so he considered it a good sign. Maybe it meant he would also fleece him for Sabrina.

Lady Sabrina Hamilton. It had a nice ring to it.

"You're quite lucky at cards. Too bad you were so unlucky with Acton," he snarked at me.

"Ha-ha. We'll see who wins out in the end," Theo said to him.

"Care to wager?" he asked with a facetious smile.

"Still no." Theo looked up as their mistresses walked into the club, doubtless assuming they'd be there.

Angeline came over and tried to sit in Theo's lap, but he shook his head at her. "My dear," he said as Mary sat on Callum's lap. "I believe we need to part ways."

Both women raised an eyebrow at him. Theo pulled out his wallet and gave Angeline several pound notes. "Here. To cover your expenses until you find another."

She looked down at the notes in her hands, shocked. Then her surprise melted into a soft smile. "You've found a high society lady. Was it love at first sight? It must have been. We were together just last evening."

"It was. And I won't taint our courtship, even with a woman as lovely as you." Theo gently pinched her cheek. "I wish you well, Angeline."

"It was fun. You're a good man. She's lucky to have you," she replied.

"She doesn't have him yet," Callum interjected, patting Mary's backside as she sat on his knee. "We're vying for the affections of the same woman."

Mary's laugh was cacophonous as always, but she had a good heart, and Callum assured me she was excellent in the bedroom. "Oh my. Who's winning?" she asked.

"It's up for debate," Theo reluctantly admitted. "The lady in question has a greater regard for me, but I managed to insult her brother. The brother, who will make the ultimate decision, is more enamored of Callum. But the game is not over."

Angeline gave him a sympathetic pat on the shoulder. "If Callum does win her, keep me in mind, lover." She nodded to Callum and Mary, then excused herself.

"You've managed to upset the brother? That's not starting ahead. I'm sure Callum will win." Mary batted her eyelashes at him. "I hope wedded bliss will not interfere with *our* arrangement."

"I don't see why it should," he replied, and Theo frowned at him.

"What?" he said, catching his gaze. "It's not as though a young virgin is as entertaining as our Mary here."

"Your Mary," Theo corrected him. "And I do think a man should eschew his mistress when he has a wife."

He chuckled. "Taking the moral high ground, I see. I won't be 'eschewing' Mary. There are some vigorous activities that a wife should not have to bear."

"I will keep the moral high ground and give up any activities that might offend my love," Theo said.

"Oh-ho. I suppose you think I'm some sort of Lothario now," Callum grinned.

He did not smile back. "I'm being serious, Tennant. A man should not shame his wife."

"There is no shame in attending one's baser instincts with a woman built to handle them," he said, patting Mary on the bottom again. "And what if gambling offends your wife? Will you give that up as well?"

"Yes," Theo said without hesitation.

Callum blinked at him. "Hamilton, you are a better man than I."

"I think you should discuss your tastes with your wife before assuming you do not have common appetites," he explained.

"And if you do not?" Callum asked.

Theo shrugged. "I may ask her if it is all right if I have a mistress, but I will not seek one out behind her back."

Callum nodded slowly. "I think Miss Acton is one who understands how the world works and would not begrudge me a mistress."

"I, for one, certainly hope not," Mary piped up. "I very much enjoy our time together, Duke Tennant."

"I enjoy it as well, Mary," he replied with a smile.

"What if you really, truly loved a woman, and she asked you to stop seeing mistresses?" Theo asked.

He furrowed his brow in thought. "I cannot see myself really, truly loving a woman. She would have to be truly extraordinary. If I met such a woman, and I did really, truly love her, I suppose I would eschew my mistress. Miss Acton is the closest yet to my ideal wife. I do not expect to find another superior to her in my estimation."

"At least I know I need not worry," Mary simpered.

"You never need worry, my flower. Even if we parted, I would ensure you were well taken care of," he said.

She laid a hand on his chest. "I am glad of that. You are a good man, Duke Tennant. I wish you nothing but goodness in your life. But you are right, knowing you, I also know there is no woman in the world who could meet your lofty criteria."

"Miss Acton meets all of mine," Theo responded confidently.

"You cannot possibly know that yet," Callum said.

"I can. I do. And I will have her." He stood. "I wish both of you a lovely evening of 'vigorous activities,' but I'm afraid I must retire."

Callum counted out my winnings and handed them to me. "I am not a bad man, Hamilton."

"No," He replied, pocketing his winnings. "Just the wrong man for Miss Acton."

The Well Dries Up

Sam

The invitations stopped coming, as Theo predicted.

"I'm sorry," Sam said to Sabrina as they sat together in the parlor, waiting for suitors to call. "It appears I did ruin your chances."

"Not at all," she replied. "I am quite happy with how things have turned out. In fact, I could do with one less suitor."

"Sabrina, it is impossible to fall in love in the span of an evening," she chided her. "Give both men a chance. Tennant has a higher rank, more land, and more income."

She bristled. "Hamilton's rank, land, and income are perfectly sufficient."

"Tennant also has better connections," Sam continued. "I am not opposed to choosing Hamilton, if he is who you truly want, but I refuse to lose a good prospect because you had two pleasant dances with a man."

"You're just angry about his bringing up your scars and pressing you to dance with a lady or two," she sniffed. "Really, Sam, you must have known your scars would be the topic of a little gossip at least. I know that's why we never leave Acton."

It stung, and she winced.

Her sister bowed her head in contrition, taking her left hand, which was her burned arm. "I know it makes you uncomfortable. I'm sorry."

"I'm always afraid if someone looks too closely at us together, they will surmise the truth," Sam confessed. "And I don't want to court a woman. It would be a lie and terribly unfair to her."

"Dancing is not courting, Sam," she reminded her.

"You managed to get two suitors out of it, even with my faux pas with Duke FitzRoy," Sam pointed out.

Sabrina's brow furrowed. "Hmm. I suppose that's true."

"I'd call that the final proof I have no place on the ballroom floor," Sam said.

"But you dance so divinely. With me, at least."

She chuckled. "I'm glad you think so, but we were the only partners available for those dance lessons."

"That's because we never leave the estate, even to see our neighbors at smaller gatherings. Sam, you've been a man almost all your life. There was never any risk," she said.

She sighed. "I do not like the idea of pretending to good friends. I believe they would deserve the truth."

"And Tennant?" Sabrina asked carefully. "I know you are forming a fast friendship with him."

Sam rubbed the bridge of her nose. "If you marry, I will, of course, not deny him the truth. If you do not, I suppose we will exchange letters as I have no intention of leaving the estate again. In letters, it will be possible to continue to conceal the truth."

"What happens when I marry Hamilton?" she responded.

A glower came over Sam's face, and he gave Sabrina a hard look. "Let us not get ahead of ourselves."

Exasperated, she let out a sigh. "All right. What happens *if* I marry Hamilton?"

"I haven't quite decided that yet. He seems to be a good sort but a man who puts his foot in it. I believe he might unintentionally reveal the truth in the wrong setting, and then where would I be?" Sam said.

"Living with me at Kilgore," Sabrina suggested. "See? Nothing too terrible."

"God only knows what Jeremy will do if I'm found out. I imagine myself brought before the court for something." She shuddered at the thought.

She frowned in confusion. "You think there is a penalty for masquerading as a man all this time?"

"I'm not entirely certain, but I wouldn't be surprised," Sam replied. "At any rate, I'm sure there would be legal repercussions for keeping Acton from Jeremy all these years when he was the rightful heir."

"Jeremy doesn't deserve Acton," Sabrina said harshly. "He will only whip the servants and discharge the poor."

"I agree." Sam squeezed her hands. "And that is why it is so important that we share my secret only with people we can trust."

"Hamilton is Tennant's best friend. You don't think Callum would tell Theo, regardless?" she asked.

Sam thought about that for a while. "I think Tennant would keep my secret, even from Hamilton."

"I don't think Hamilton is as faithless as you believe him to be. He had an error in judgment. But his heart is good, and he would make an excellent brother-in-law," she said.

"And an excellent husband is where I suppose you are going with this," Sam sighed. "All right, I will give him his fair chance."

Sabrina smiled and gave me a hug. "Thank you, sister of mine. That's all I ask."

She shook her head, already thinking she was going to regret giving Theo a second chance. But for Sabrina, Sam would do just about anything.

A chime rang, and soon a maid came into the parlor holding two calling cards. "His Grace Callum Tennant, Duke of Conford has come to call, as well as Lord Theodore Hamilton of Kilgore. Shall I show them in?"

"Yes, please!" Sabrina cried.

The maid, unmoved, continued to direct her attention at Sam. "Yes, of course. Thank you, Anne."

Anne nodded and went to show the men in.

Theo came in first, his smile sparkling in the sunlight along with his dark blond hair. Both women stood, and Sam bowed while Sabrina curtsied. "Welcome to our London home, Hamilton," Sam said politely.

"Thank you for so kindly allowing me to call," Theo replied.

"And me as well," Callum added, entering the parlor.

Sam's breath caught when she saw him. He was even more impressive in the daylight. The women bowed and curtsied again.

Unused to these strange feelings Callum was inspiring in her, Sam tamped down on them mercilessly. She suspected she might regard him a little more than she should, and following that to its conclusion would be disastrous for everyone.

"Do sit down," Sabrina beamed, gesturing to the chairs across from the small settee where the women sat. She was a very good hostess, despite a lack of opportunities to show off her skills.

Both men sat, Theo wearing a genuine, bright smile while Callum's was more sardonic. He found the social graces just as idiotic as Sam did Another thing they could agree on.

"Are you going to the Morgans' ball?" Theo asked, his eyes entirely fixated on Sabrina.

Her smile faltered, and Sam resisted the urge to roll his eyes. Theo just couldn't stop putting his foot in it, for some reason. "I'm afraid we weren't invited," Sabrina responded sadly.

"Invitations dried up. I knew it." Theo shook his head. "That's a very great shame. I shall have to take you for a walk in the park sometime." He suddenly looked at Sam. "If that is amenable to you, of course."

"I have already decided my social faux pas and the prevailing gossip about my... condition... should not impede my lovely sister from enjoying the delights of London," she replied stiffly. "I'm sure I will turn some heads, but that is no reason for me to refuse to chaperone my sister on an outing to the park."

Sabrina put a hand on her knee. "You don't have to, Sam. Really. I'm just as content to meet here."

"What my bumbling friend here is suggesting is perhaps a nice outing for all of us," Callum inserted. "I think, between the four of us, we can get the tongues to stop wagging."

"Or wag more," Theo grinned.

Callum put a hand to his forehead. "Hamilton."

He seemed to remember himself and blushed. "I apologize, I was just making a little joke."

"I'm sure it's a very funny one," Sam said. "I just fail to see the humor." She shrugged. "I suppose that must mean it was at my expense."

"Theo doesn't mean anything by it. To be blunt, he and I both think it's silly that you've become such a topic of conversation. Your scars are not noticeable enough to deter any young lady, I wouldn't think. And that is why Hamilton is being so awkward. He doesn't really see you as I think you see yourself," Callum responded delicately.

"It's a very sensitive subject." Sabrina waved a hand. "Let us discuss something else."

Sam smiled slightly at his sister. "Perhaps politics?"

She groaned. "Perhaps not. I'd have thought you'd gotten your fill of that last night!"

Sam glanced at Callum, who was looking at her with a knowing twinkle in his eye. "Can one ever really tire of talking about politics? There is so much ground to cover," he said. "But I'm glad you didn't just smile and nod, sitting there with a glazed look in your eyes while the rest of us discussed a subject you are weary of speaking about."

Sabrina blushed. "Sam encourages me to have my own opinions and to let my wants and needs be known."

"That's wonderful," the men said together.

She put a hand to her mouth to cover a laugh. "Oh dear. I'm spoiled for compliments today."

"As well you should be," Theo insisted.

Sam bit his lip against a smile at both men vying for my sister's attention. "I believe Sabrina to be worthy of all the best compliments."

Callum's lips twitched. He'd caught on to the facetiousness in Sam's tone.

"Why don't we discuss poetry?" her sister suggested.

It was Sam's turn for an inward groan. Of course, she was versed in Shakespeare and had a passing familiarity with the popular poets of the day, but it wasn't a favorite subject of hers. "Yes," she said, trying to sound as enthusiastic as possible. "Let's."

Callum coughed to cover a laugh.

Theo and Sabrina were in their own little world, however, and didn't notice.

"I suppose you have many interesting opinions on Shakespeare?" Callum asked, trying to keep his laughter under control.

"I've always been especially fond of his historical plays," Sam replied. "But I suppose we are meant to be discussing the sonnets."

"We could always discuss Shelley," Sabrina said, still the good hostess though she gave Sam's foot an annoyed little tap at her mocking of her topic.

"Oh, I quite like 'Ozymandias,'" Callum responded. "I like how it tells a story of how all empires, no matter how great, will one day be nothing but sand."

"I suppose Britain will be that way someday," Sam agreed. "I only hope we leave a positive imprint on the world. Perhaps like the Greeks of old."

"The way things are going now with our poor, well, it seems highly unlikely we will be remembered fondly," Callum grumbled.

"Perhaps remembered fondly by the Americans," Sam said.

Sabrina sighed, and she realized they'd gone off on the topic of politics again.

"It is a lovely day, Sabrina," Theo interrupted what Sam was sure was going to be a great debate about the colonies. "Shall we go to the balcony and see the hustle and bustle?"

"Yes," she replied, rising. "I would be most grateful for the distraction."

Theo offered her his arm while Sam mouthed a quick, "My apologies," to her.

She merely shrugged and smiled at Theo as he escorted her out onto the balcony affixed to the parlor. As was proper, he kept himself and Sabrina in Sam's line of sight.

"I don't suppose I shall ever win her over," Callum chuckled.

"Well, you've won me over, and that's a good start," she said. "You just need to spend more time with her. Perhaps without Hamilton hanging on."

"Good point. But I'm afraid that won't happen. We made each other a promise on the way here that one of us would not visit Sabrina without the other. Though I'm beginning to think that's working more in Hamilton's favor." He gave Sam a self-deprecating smile.

"For a man as intelligent as you are, that was a rather unintelligent agreement on your part," she laughed lightly.

"True." He leaned forward in his chair. "Now, about the colonies..."

Out on the Balcony

Sabrina

"I hope I wasn't too forward, assuming you wanted to be rescued from their conversation," Theo said as we stood out on the balcony.

"Not at all," Sabrina replied. "You read the situation quite well. I was hoping to be rescued."

"Good," he smiled. "I've always wanted to be a white knight."

"And today you got your chance." Sabrina grinned up at him. "Does that make me a princess?"

He laughed. "I like that much more than 'damsel in distress.' It's more fitting."

"Well, I was in distress." Sabrina looked down at the people walking below. Most were wearing fine clothes, but there was the odd street urchin or flower seller.

"No, my lady, *I* was the one in distress. If Tennant was going to start in on the subject of the colonies, it would have been terribly dull," Theo responded.

Sabrina smiled. "Then, I must find myself a white horse."

"You would look resplendent on a white horse." The expression on Theo's face made her blood heat up, and she knew she was blushing.

His expression grew even softer. "You look quite fine today, Miss Acton."

"Thank you. You look quite fine as well. My, is it hot outside?" she commented, trying to pass off her deepening blush on the weather.

"It must be." He nodded, taking the pressure off her. "Those are some very lovely flowers in that woman's cart down there. Shall I buy you some?"

"Not if it means you would leave me with those two." Sabrina made a face. "I don't think I could bear talking about the state of international trade."

Theo put on an innocent face, though his lips threatened to curl up into a smile. "But they may start speaking about the strength of the British pound. Would you want to miss that?"

She groaned. "Yes, please."

"I promise, I shall not leave your side for a moment." Theo put a hand over his heart.

"I don't mind that one bit," Sabrina replied softly.

"Good."

After a few moments of comfortable silence, Sabrina could see Theo was casting about for polite conversation, so she decided to help him. "Is Kilgore nice this time of year?"

"Quite," he replied, relieved. "I keep lovely gardens, and they will be in full bloom about now. Unfortunately, I tend to spend most of my time in London, so I do not get to enjoy them as much as I'd like to."

"A great pity," she said.

"And Acton? Do you miss it? It must also be beautiful this time of year." Theo's eyes were a warm brown and Sabrina sank into them, feeling as though she might be lost forever.

"Hmm?" she asked when his eyes crinkled at the corners with a wide smile.

"Acton," he prompted.

Sabrina felt herself blush again. "Forgive me, my mind must have been elsewhere. I love Acton. I spent all my life there. In fact, I haven't been to London since I was four years old."

"Oh my. You do have some catching up to do," Theo said. "I must then insist we take a walk in the park. I don't think your brother will be too inconvenienced."

Her eyebrows drew together. "I worry about the gossips. Especially after what happened at the ball."

"Gossips will gossip; there's no help for that. Every one of us is a subject of gossip at one time or another. You simply haven't been in London long enough to acquaint yourself with the workings of society," he replied.

"Yes. My brother found that out rather early. I suppose we seem like country bumpkins now," she sighed.

"I don't see you that way. Either of you. And Tennant thinks your brother is delightful," Theo said.

Sabrina smiled. "Sam is delightful. You two simply got off on the wrong foot."

"Obviously. I suppose, if I am to be a serious suitor, I should go back in there and try to engage Acton in some sort of political discourse." Theo sounded infinitely bored by this prospect.

"Don't bother. Those two will never let you get a word in." Sabrina looked back into the parlor and shook her head. "Not one word."

Theo laughed. "I would have to agree with you, Miss Acton."

Sabrina bit her lip. "Is it too soon to ask you to call me Miss Sabrina?"

His eyes lit up. "I am honored... Miss Sabrina."

She gave him a delighted smile.

"Unfortunately, decorum keeps me from asking you to simply call me Hamilton, but that day will come in time," he replied.

A blush crept into Sabrina's cheeks. "I hope not too long a time."

He laughed. "A man could easily forget himself with you. Your brother would likely throw me off this balcony if I was so forward after two days."

"Sam? He would simply challenge you to fisticuffs and leave you a bleeding mess," she said.

Theo began to laugh, then stopped. "You're serious."

She nodded. "Sam is awfully talented in many areas, not the least of which being fisticuffs. But worse yet, he would deny you coming to call anymore. And that would be a great shame."

"It would," Theo agreed. "Though I am determined to take you to the park."

Sabrina shifted uncomfortably. "While I would love to go to the park with you, I do worry about my brother. Especially after the Barrington's Ball."

"I suppose he was too self-conscious to go to Eton or Harrow as well," he lamented.

"We had a perfectly good governess and he learned as much if not more than he would have at Eton or Harrow," she replied defensively.

"Oh, no doubt. He's holding his own with Tennant," Theo said quickly. "It is simply a shame we did not get to know him when we were boys in school."

"Duke Tennant and you went to Harrow, then?" she asked.

He shook his head. "Eton."

"Was it nice?" she continued politely.

"Boarding schools are rarely 'nice,' Miss Sabrina. But it does forge fast friendships," he said. "And if your brother's fists are as fearsome as you say, he would have had no trouble there."

"Hmm." She was unconvinced, but for reasons Theo was, of course, unaware of.

He sighed. "Change of subject, then. Why don't we all go to the opera? They are putting on *The Marriage of Figaro* right now. The theater will be suitably dark. No one will stare at your brother."

Sabrina brightened. "Oh, that sounds like a lovely idea. Sam and I have never been to the opera. I've always wanted to see one."

"It's settled then. I shall beg an evening of your brother, and we shall all go to see *The Marriage of Figaro*. Do you know Italian?"

"Yes. And French," she responded proudly. "And Latin. Sam got it into his head that he also wanted to learn Greek, but I stopped at Latin."

"He probably wanted to read the great philosophers in their mother tongue," he suggested.

"Yes, that would make sense." She was about to say more, but just then, a carriage came careening down Charles Place. "Oh my! Someone's going to get hurt! What is he thinking, driving that horse at that speed?!"

Theo leaned over the rail as the carriage knocked over the flower lady and crashed right into her cart, finally coming to a stop. "The harness is broken. Once he has fixed it, we shall have to go down and purchase that poor woman's flowers. Doubtless the driver will reimburse her for the damage done to her c—"

The driver got down from the cart and began beating his horse mercilessly with a whip. The flower lady came over to make her complaints known, and he beat her as well, along with two urchins who had been hiding behind her cart. Sabrina wondered if they were her children.

Sabrina's hands flew to her mouth, and Theo quickly took her arm and turned her away. "This is no sight for a lady. Tennant! There's a problem on the street. We must address it immediately!"

Callum stood, and so did Sam. "What problem?"

Theo pointed to the balcony while he ushered Sabrina away from it.

Sam and Callum rushed to see, then both let out cries of protest. "You down there! Stop that!" Sam yelled.

The driver ignored them.

The two men and Sam hurried outside with Sabrina in their wake. Callum made straight for the driver, catching his wrist on a down-swing and squeezing until the driver dropped the whip. Sam went to the horse to calm it while Theo and Sabrina ran straight to the flower lady and her two children.

Callum shook the driver until his teeth rattled, pointing out what a disgusting excuse for a human being he was. Under Sam's care, the horse calmed to a few twitching grunts.

Sabrina dabbed at the bleeding children's faces with her own sleeve, ignoring whatever bloodstains were ruining her dress. Theo had taken off his coat and wrapped it around the flower lady's shoulders. The woman burst into grateful tears.

"We must bring them inside," Sabrina insisted. "Their wounds need treating."

"Yes, we must," Theo agreed.

One of the household staff came to relieve Sam of the horse and take it away, making the driver squawk.

Callum held the now quite pale driver so he was nose-to-nose with him. "If I were you, I would start walking back the way you came."

"But my horse, the carriage..." the driver whined.

Callum reached into his jacket and pulled out his pocketbook. He peeled off several pound notes and shoved them into the driver's pocket. "I suggest you forget them both. Now walk."

The driver nodded vigorously and not only walked, but ran back the way he had come.

Once that was settled, the four escorted the flower woman and her children inside Eleven Charles Place.

"Anne, do bring some tea and something to eat," Sabrina said as they all entered. "And tell the steward to bring a wound kit."

Anne curtsied. "At once, Miss Acton." She went to do just that.

Sabrina got all three of their new guests seated in the parlor.

The flower woman looked horrified when she saw her children were bleeding on the settee. "Madam, your furniture!"

"Hush. No one cares about the furniture right now," Sabrina assured her. She waved the steward over when he came in and started carefully cleaning their wounds.

Anne arrived not long after with tea and an assortment of nibbles. "Please, help yourselves," Sabrina said to the flower woman and the two children.

The two children dove right in while the flower woman was more reserved. "Be polite. Don't make no mess," she whispered to her children.

Sabrina could tell the woman and her children were very hungry, and her heart ached for them. "How long have you been selling flowers?" she asked.

"Was me first day, madam. Scrimped and saved we did so's we could have a better life. Now it's all ruined," the flower woman said sadly.

"No. We won't let it all go to ruin. Don't you worry. Sam, what do you suppose it would cost to get her started again?" she asked.

Sam was just reaching for her pocketbook when Theo stopped her. "I insist." He produced a generous number of pound notes and the flower woman's eyes widened.

"Cor, now, it weren't *that* costly," she protested.

Theo pressed the money into her freshly-bandaged hands. "It takes a little time to get a business up and running. This is so you can eat and sleep somewhere decent in the meantime."

The flower woman's eyes filled with tears. "Bless you, my lord. Bless you. 'Tis sure God sent you to us. All of you."

"Do you have somewhere to sleep tonight?" Sabrina asked worriedly.

"Oh, yes, madam. We share with my sister'n hers." She stood, waving at her children to do the same. "We'll go there now. May the good Lord bless you all."

"Safe travels," Sabrina said as Anne showed the three of them out.

Good Company

Callum

"That is precisely why attitudes about the poor need to change," Sam said angrily as the flower woman and her children left.

"Indeed," Callum agreed. "But as long as the Tories are in power, I fear we shall always see incidents like this swept under the rug."

"Before we get too deep into politics," Theo interrupted. "I was just saying to Miss Acton how we should all go see *The Marriage of Figaro*. It's playing at the Theatre Royal."

Callum raised an eyebrow. "You've given up on your walk in the park?"

"No, not yet." Theo glanced uncomfortably at Sam, and Callum understood the path of his logic.

"It will be quite dark in there," Callum murmured quietly to Sam. "Gossip abounds before, after, and during intermissions, however, we shall be quite safe during the performance itself."

Sam huffed a sigh. "I appreciate your concern for my comfort, but if I am only traveling to London with my sister once, I must endure."

"Not a fan of the opera?" Callum asked.

"They've never been," Theo replied instead of Sam.

"But we must. We must see at least one. Can we? Please, Sam?" Sabrina begged.

Sam's features softened, and Callum realized Sam would do anything for his sister. "Of course. It sounds like a lovely evening. When is the next performance?"

"Tonight," Theo said eagerly. "If that is not too soon, of course."

"Sam wanted to be out of London with me properly engaged in a week. I doubt anything is too soon," Sabrina teased.

He just shook his head indulgently. "Tonight seems a fine night."

"I don't usually get caught up in many of London's diversions when it comes to the arts," Callum admitted. "But opera is a rare exception. I'm sure you will both love it."

"I'm sure we will!" Sabrina replied excitedly.

Sam did not look quite as convinced, but Callum knew seeing it for himself would bring him around.

"We should bid you adieu for now. I'm sure Miss Acton has much to do to prepare. Ladies always do." Callum winked.

"It's expected," Sabrina pointed out. "I would not shame you by showing up in a flour sack."

Callum and Theo both laughed. "Please, do not! It would cause *such* a scandal!" Theo said.

"I believe I've already contributed enough to that for the both of us," Sam added ruefully.

Sabrina smiled and curtsied while Sam and the two visitors bowed. "I have enjoyed your visit very much. I look forward to tonight's plans."

"We do as well, Miss Sabrina," Theo grinned back.

Why that sneaky little bastard. "Miss... Sabrina?" Callum echoed.

Sam did not look very happy about the situation. "I suppose, if you are both courting her, you may as well call her Miss Sabrina," he said in a tight tone.

"But—!" Sabrina began.

"Miss Sabrina it is, then," Callum responded, trying to hide his smile at Theo's and Sabrina's looks of righteous indignation.

"We will see you this evening," Sam continued. "It's been a pleasure. Hamilton. Tennant."

A part of Callum rather liked the way Sam said his name, which surprised him because, though opportunities abounded at Eton, Callum had never had the impulse to bugger a boy. His eyebrows drew together, but Theo managed to rescue him this time by grabbing him by the arm and dragging him out.

"You seemed to be stuck," Theo said when we were out on the street.

"I was. Thank you." He fiddled with his cravat, trying to think of why his pulse had fluttered when Sam said his name.

"Now you look as though someone walked over your grave." Theo frowned, concerned.

"Do Acton and Miss Sabrina sound alike?" Callum grasped at explanations.

Theo looked thoughtful. "I suppose they do, a bit. Though Acton's voice is a bit more gravelly. Doubtless because he is a man."

"Doubtless." Callum was still troubled.

"Or, it could have been the fire," Theo suggested.

"That is also possible." Callum began to walk more quickly, feeling a bit suffocated.

Theo quickened his steps to keep up. "Tennant, are you well?"

"No. I need to get home," he replied.

With a grin, Theo teased, "Are you going to allow me to escort Miss Sabrina without you, then?"

That snapped Callum right back into reality. "Never."

"I thought not," he said. He clapped Callum on the shoulder. "What is bothering you?"

"I can hardly confess it to myself. No, do not ask. I will confide in you if and when I feel the time is right," Callum murmured.

Theo raised his eyebrows at his friend. "It must be grave, indeed. I will stop asking."

"Thank you," he said.

❧

MERCIFULLY, BY THE TIME THEY ARRIVED BACK AT ELEVEN Charles Place in a carriage to pick up Sam and Sabrina, Callum had managed to explain away his strange feelings. He blamed them entirely on Theo's having suggested he bugger Sam the night of the Barrington's Ball. That and Sam's strikingly similar appearance to Sabrina.

When Sam and Sabrina exited their house, Callum was sure he'd have no more inappropriate thoughts about Sam. Indeed, the man was smartly-dressed, and as like his sister as ever, but Callum was much more interested in his mind than his body. That had to be it. The Greeks and Romans had found a marriage of minds between men and taken that to a physical conclusion. Perhaps, having finally met his match, Callum had found his Roman side.

At any rate, it mattered little. Sabrina was who he was courting. He needed to pry her out of Theo's hands.

Sam helped her up into the carriage, and she immediately looked disappointed that Callum and Theo were both sitting on the same side. Doubtless, she'd wanted to sit next to Theo.

Callum resolved to be charm itself. Theo might have her attention now, but he was determined to win it in the end.

"You look well, Miss Sabrina," Callum said before Theo could.

"Yes, indeed," Theo added, late on the draw.

Sabrina smiled at them both, and Callum felt a warmth in his chest. He enjoyed her smile very much. "Thank you both," she replied.

"You're welcome," Theo and Callum said together.

Sam looked out the window immediately after sitting down, a hand at his mouth, and Callum could tell he was trying not to laugh at this delicate dance the two men and his sister were doing. It made Callum smile.

Perhaps if Sabrina did end up marrying Theo, he would still find some excuse to see Sam at Acton, or perhaps some time in London would soften Sam enough that he would consider visiting at Conford. It was a terrible shame that Jeremy Acton, the louse, had decided to throw his cousin to the rumor mill. Speculating about the man's scarring was bad enough without outright questioning his manhood.

If he'd been an Eton man, he certainly would have beaten the impertinence out of his cousin. However, Sam's sheltered existence must necessarily have made him sensitive to the gossip of the ton. Perhaps his father had been ashamed of him?

Callum shook his head, trying not to speculate himself. Though he would never share his theories with anyone but Theo, he still felt he was doing Sam a disservice by picking apart the topic at all, even in his mind.

The carriage rolled through the London streets to Covent Garden. Callum had secured his usual box for the occasion, and they were quickly ushered there by helpful staff.

Sabrina stared about her in awe, tugging on her brother's arm and pointing at this fresco and that chandelier.

Sam, on the other hand, was looking around at the crowd who, as feared, were whispering to each other while they passed. He tugged his collar points a bit higher and ducked his head, as though he could retract it into his neck like a tortoise.

Callum wanted to give them all a sound beating. "This is one of my favorites," he told Sam to distract him from the gossips. "*The Marriage of Figaro* must be one of Mozart's best. It's a comedy. You'll enjoy it."

His new friend forced a smile, and Callum's heart ached for him. "I'm sure I shall enjoy it very much."

"Don't pay them any attention," Theo added and Callum began to wonder if he'd been born with one wit in his head. "They don't know you, and you don't know them. They are the ones being rude."

Next thing, Theo was going to start talking about Sam's scars again. "Why don't you take Miss Sabrina ahead for a bit, Hamilton? She seems to be completely enamored by the theatre."

"But not out of my sight," Sam inserted quickly.

Theo looked delighted, as did Sabrina. He offered Sabrina his arm, which she took, and they walked ahead of Callum and Sam.

"Walk with your head held high," Callum whispered to Sam. "Remember you are the man who told Duke FitzRoy how inane his views on the poor are. You are still that man, Acton."

Sam looked up at him for a moment. Then he squared his shoulders and poked his chin back out of his collar.

"That's better." Callum clapped Sam on the shoulder and they walked more easily side-by-side.

When they arrived at Callum's box, Theo insisted Sabrina sit in one of the front two seats. He was about to take the other when Callum shook his head sharply.

"Acton, as this is your first opera performance, I insist you sit next to your sister," he said. "You must be as close to the stage as possible."

"Thank you," Sam replied, taking the seat next to Sabrina, who looked disappointed once more.

"You really are a pain," Theo muttered as he and Callum sat down behind them.

Callum snorted. "I was about to say the same about you."

He would have responded to his barb, Callum was sure, if the lights had not begun to lower. Soon, the curtain drew up.

Figaro and Suzanna began the piece, talking about their wedding to come and their new room. Suzanna, maid to the countess, warned that the count had been making advances on her and intended to exert his right of first bedding, as she was a servant of his household. Figaro hatched a plan to embarrass the count to keep that from happening.

It was an opera Callum enjoyed, but as he had seen it before, he took pleasure instead in watching Sabrina's and Sam's reactions to it.

At first, it seemed the two of them were enjoying themselves.

Then, when Cherubino came onstage and began to sing of his love of all women, especially the countess, both siblings stiffened.

Callum couldn't understand why. Cherubino was one of the funniest roles in the entire production—a breeches role of some renown. A man played by a beautiful soprano woman, Cherubino only became funnier as the opera went on. At one point, the woman dressed as a man then dressed as a woman to deceive the count, but was unsuccessful. Knowing Cherubino's actor was actually a woman just made the situation all the more hilarious.

However, from the time Cherubino showed up on the scene, Sabrina and Sam both seemed uncomfortable. At first, they very pointedly did not look at each other. Then they shared worried glances.

By Act Two, Callum began to suspect something was very wrong. "Acton? Miss Sabrina? Are you well?" he whispered.

Their heads whipped around, and Callum got the feeling he'd caught them at something. But Sabrina quickly put a hand to her head. "I'm afraid I'm feeling a bit faint. Don't mind me, please. It's just the vapors. Sam is just worried about me."

Callum didn't believe her for a moment, especially considering how pale Sam had become. If something was wrong, it was with the brother, not the sister. "Perhaps we should leave at the end of Act Two? If you are feeling unwell."

Sabrina looked at Sam, and then Callum was sure of it. It was Sam who was in some sort of secret distress.

"No," Sam said. "We have come to see the opera, and we will see the opera. If that is all right with you, Sabrina."

Her expression said it was anything but all right, but she plastered on a smile and nodded. "Yes. I'm sure I'll feel much better in a moment or two."

"Are you sure?" Theo asked worriedly, joining our conversation.

"Of course," Sabrina smiled weakly.

Cherubino

Sabrina

After the entrance of Cherubino, the entire opera was agony.

Sabrina was sure it was a lovely opera, that the voices were pure and the different foibles of the characters suitably humorous, but seeing the woman dressed as a man had thrown both Sam and her. Cherubino's very presence made it impossible to enjoy the rest of the opera. Sabrina was sure Sam was worried about being found out even more than she was worried about her sister's secret being revealed. After all, it would take little imagination to make the connection.

Sam looked very much like Sabrina, even with short hair and a burn scar on the side of her face.

All through the opera, she wanted to hold Sam's hand to comfort her. But that would have been a very telling gesture.

Callum was also far too perceptive. While Sabrina had made an excuse about the vapors, she knew he didn't believe her. That being said, by the end of the opera, Sabrina was feeling faint from the stress.

Sam, always attentive, recognized Sabrina's distress and had her arm handy when it was time for them to stand and clap. Of course, the cast had been so good it warranted three standing ovations, even while Sabrina was hoping to just leave.

When the audience did begin to exit, she picked up her skirts, ready to run out of the theatre, but the two men were there, eyeing them curiously.

"Did something in the production offend you?" Theo asked.

"Do you still have the vapors?" Callum added with a smirk.

"Someone's perfume," Sam saved Sabrina from answering. "It's making her feel ill."

"Oh, that's a shame. It was a very good production," Theo said. "Let's get you out of here."

Sam transferred her from her arm to Theo's. Sabrina saw her sister was still pale, and subtly squeezed her hand as Theo began to walk her out.

Callum was already staring Sam up and down, and Sabrina desperately wanted to go back to her sister to protect her, but supposed it was best that one of them got out of there before their secret was revealed.

"I'm sorry you had such a poor experience," Theo said again as they walked among the crowd leaving the theatre. Sabrina had never been so frustrated with people ambulating aimlessly in her entire life. Didn't people have places to go?!

She forced a smile and fanned herself a bit. "I'm sure it was a lovely opera. We shall have to go again, perhaps to a different production? The same woman cannot possibly show up twice."

"She very well could. I think the open air of the park would be best for now. Tomorrow, do you suppose?" Theo asked. "I know you worry about your brother, so if the suggestion is offensive to you..."

"We will take a turn about the park tomorrow," Sam confirmed as she and Callum caught up to them. Her ears were pink and Callum's cheeks were ruddy. Had they fought?

Sabrina shot Callum a questioning glance, but his green eyes revealed nothing.

"That's wonderful!" Theo exclaimed, and his happiness was

infectious. She smiled up at him, forgetting, for a moment, that Sam and Callum were cross.

Now that she was in a better mood, Sabrina felt sad when the carriage came. It meant she had little time left to spend with Theo.

But, happily, it was he who gave her a hand up into the carriage and not Sam this time.

Sam did take the seat next to her, however, and she and Callum were noticeably silent the entire ride back to Eleven Charles Place. Even Theo looked from Callum, to Sam, and back again in confusion. But he did not comment, and Sabrina thought it wise that she didn't either.

The carriage rolled to a stop at their door and this time Callum got out to help Sabrina down. She gave him a pleasant smile. "Thank you for the lovely evening," she said.

He smirked. "You're a much better liar than your brother."

So it was still 'brother.' Sabrina felt her breath finally return. "Well, one of us has to be," Sabrina replied with a cheeky grin.

Callum threw his head back and laughed, though he pointedly did not look at Sam as she got down from the carriage and held out her arm to her.

"Good evening, Tennant, Hamilton," Sam said crisply, giving a slight bow to each.

"Acton," Callum responded, then hopped back into the carriage and told the driver to move on before Theo could say a thing.

Sabrina remained silent until they entered the townhome. Once the door closed behind them, however, she rounded on Sam. "What has happened between you and Duke Tennant?!"

"As he said, I am a poor liar," she evaded, handing her coat to Anne.

"Tosh. You've been a man for thirteen years. You're an excellent liar," Sabrina said.

"Our secret is safe, that is all you need to know," her sister assured her.

She followed Sam into the parlor just the same. "Something has happened. You were such friends. You have so few, Sam, I hate to see you lose one."

Sam sighed. "He asked me what was wrong with the performance and I think I mumbled something about being afraid of heights, but he told me that was utter rubbish."

"He didn't say 'rubbish' did he," Sabrina surmised.

"He said something a lady need not hear. At any rate, he was quite angry with me because I would say no more on the subject." Sam collapsed into a chair and covered her face with her hand.

Sabrina pulled an ottoman over next to her sister to sit down and put a hand on her arm. "You are still friends, though."

"I'm not terribly clear on that point," Sam said.

"Oh Sam. I'm sorry." Sabrina waved to Anne. "Please bring tea."

"Cognac would be better," Sam grumped.

"Tea, Anne," Sabrina said firmly.

Anne nodded and, for once, did Sabrina's bidding instead of Sam's, coming back with tea and not cognac.

The sisters shared tea in silence for a while, then Sam sighed again. "This is why I don't leave Acton."

"I'm proud of you for doing so, Sam," Sabrina rejoined. "I know it's something you weren't comfortable with, but you've stretched your horizons a bit And likely have made a good friend."

"How good of a friend can he be if he never knows I'm not a man? He wouldn't be interested in political discussions with me if he knew what I really am," Sam scoffed.

"He might. Anyway, you've set your mind on my marrying one of them, so doubtless the other will know as well," Sabrina said.

"We've had this conversation. I don't trust Hamilton," she grunted.

Sabrina took a deep breath. "I do. And if I get a choice in the matter, I choose him."

"I still think it's too soon for that decision," Sam said. "I'm sorry, I know that's not what you want to hear, but I am resolved within myself to give both men a fair chance. Therefore, I would like you to do the same."

"I'm trying." Sabrina stood and began to walk around the room, wringing her hands. "A week is not long enough, Sam. Even two. And you know that. Because if it is long enough, then I've made up my mind."

"No, you're right. We must find some other way. But I cannot stay in London much longer, Sabrina. I do not like it here, and I am ever self-conscious. I wish we could continue your courtship at Acton," Sam responded.

Sabrina blinked and turned back to her sister. "Why not?"

"Why not what?" Sam asked.

"Why not have them both come stay at Acton? Then you will be among the servants, who all know who and what you are and will take great pains to keep our secret," she said.

"My secret," Sam retorted.

Sabrina walked over and took her hands. "*Our* secret. It is as much mine as it is yours. You are my sister, but have been a better brother to me than any I could have asked for, and if you willed it, I would keep our secret in my heart and never tell Hamilton. But I think you should tell Tennant. You intend to anyway if we marry."

Sam pursed her lips. "I'll think about it."

"And inviting them to Acton?" she pressed.

"I think the idea has merit. I don't want you making up your mind on the strength of two-weeks' courtship, not on either of them," Sam confessed. "And you are right. The servants will keep my secret."

"Our secret," Sabrina reminded her again.

"We can argue that later. For now, let us just say *the* secret will be kept. I shall extend the invitation to them tomorrow at the park," she said.

"Excellent." She stood and placed a kiss on the top of Sam's head. "We will both be more comfortable at home, I believe. None of these operas imitate life."

Same gave a weak smile. "I think it was meant to be humorous."

"I don't remember laughing," Sabrina said. "I shall retire for the evening. You should as well. No cognac."

"Yes, mother." Sam raised her teacup to her sister and took a large gulp.

She nodded, gathered up her skirts, and exited the parlor.

Anne helped her to undress and braided her hair, and she was soon cocooned in the sheets and duvet of a snug canopy bed. The down pillows cushioned a heavy head.

"Oh Sam," Sabrina murmured. "When will you look out for your own happiness?"

Liar, Liar

CALLUM

"Did you notice something odd about the Acton twins tonight?" Callum asked Theo as they took the carriage away from Eleven Charles Place and to their usual club.

"Yes," Theo said. "But I did not get into a fight with Acton about it."

Callum looked sharply at Theo. "You knew they were lying."

"Of course I knew." Theo rolled his eyes. "I'm not a complete idiot. Whatever it was, Miss Sabrina was trying to cover for Acton."

"That much I did ascertain, though the liar tried to spin a tale of being afraid of heights," Callum snorted.

"Maybe he is afraid of heights," Theo suggested.

"Bollocks. That man isn't afraid of anything, except something that happened in the production. As there was no fire in it, I have no idea what it could be, but I am going to find out," Callum said.

Theo groaned. "Tennant, let it go."

"I will not have my brother-in-law lie to my face!" he exploded.

"Potential brother-in-law. I do believe that I'm still in the running," Theo said.

"Whatever. Acton is a friend, and I am very disappointed that he would try to pull a ruse on me." Callum jumped down from the carriage when they arrived at the club, storming toward the entrance.

Theo ran to catch up. "Everyone has secrets, Tennant. It is unfair of you to hold him to a higher standard."

"He holds himself to a higher standard," Callum shot back.

"Ah." Theo nodded as they were seated at their usual table. "I understand it now. You don't like that your righteous Acton has fallen from his pedestal."

Callum glowered at Theo, ordering cognac for the both of them. Then he conceded the point with a tilt of his head. "I suppose I am a bit angry about that, yes. But he put himself up there. He believes in the truth. But at the first difficulty, he won't reveal it to me. It is quite vexing."

"Indeed." Theo thanked the waiter for the cognac and took a sip.

"Also, you have no secrets. You wouldn't know how to keep one if you did have one," Callum went on.

Theo chuckled. "Perhaps not. But, surely, you do."

"Are there any secrets left in London? The women of society have certainly sussed out the majority of them by now," Callum complained. He tapped his chin thoughtfully. "I suppose my one secret is my mistress. I have not told Miss Sabrina about her."

"You should," Theo remarked.

He gave Theo a sardonic smile. "You just want to have more points in your favor."

"And you are concealing something quite important from Miss Sabrina. She does not strike me as the kind of young lady who would care for her husband to have a mistress, regardless of what you say about tastes," he said.

Mary, the mistress in question, chose that moment to come sit on Callum's lap.

Callum gave her backside a little squeeze, then turned back to Theo. "I believe she is more understanding than you think."

"Why not try explaining the situation to her, then?" he asked.

"I will explain it to her after we are married," Callum grunted.

Theo's eyes narrowed. "That is terribly unfair to her."

"Hamilton, do be reasonable." Callum turned his head as Mary began to whisper something in his ear.

"He's just no fun," she said. "Let's go back to mine and make our own fun."

"I promise you, Tennant. If you don't tell her before your marriage, then I will," Theo warned.

His head snapped around. "You'll do what?!"

"If she chooses you or her brother chooses you for her, I will make sure they both know about your mistress before the wedding," Theo said.

Callum scooped Mary off his lap so he could stand and loom over Theo. "See here. No friend of mine is going to do something like that to me."

"You're angry about Sam keeping secrets, but you're keeping the most important one from his sister. And him," Theo accused. "It would be my duty as a gentleman."

"Am I to lose all my friends today?!" Callum seethed. He squeezed his eyes shut and took a deep breath. "Fine. I will tell Acton. I will leave it up to him if he decides to tell his sister or not."

"He will. Because he is a man of honor," Theo said.

Callum frowned at him. "Are you saying I am not a man of honor?"

"No, Tennant. I'm saying you were going to do something dishonorable," his friend replied. "And I was going to stop you. Now, I intend to hold you to your promise."

"I will find the right time and place." Callum took Mary by the arm. "Don't go rushing off to tell them now."

"It's the middle of the night, Tennant," Theo pointed out.

"Exactly." Callum tucked Mary's hand into his arm. "Now, if you'll excuse me, I think I will go spend some time at Mary's apartment."

Theo pressed his lips into a thin, disapproving line.

"Glad I have your approval." He walked away from Theo and out of the club, Mary happily bouncing along beside him. It wasn't far to her apartment.

The apartment was rather lavish, owing to Mary's skill both at choosing and pleasing lovers. Callum was always generous and kept her in the lifestyle to which she had become accustomed.

"More cognac, darling?" Mary asked once Callum had settled himself in a plush chair.

He shook his head, frowning slightly. Something in him was getting the feeling it was wrong to be there. He wondered if he'd brought Theo's voice with him in his pocket.

But, when Mary began to disrobe, it was not Theo who came to mind but Sam. What would Sam think of him keeping a mistress? He didn't care so much about what Sabrina thought or even Theo, but Sam's opinion meant something more somehow.

"You didn't let him get to you, did you?" Mary asked, starting to sit on his lap again, naked.

Callum sighed and waved her off. "I'm not sure. But I don't think we can do this tonight, angel." He pulled out his wallet and took out several pound notes. "Perhaps give me a week to get things sorted out, and we can revisit our arrangement."

"My poor duke," she simpered, taking the money and putting it in a covered serving dish on her table. "I think, if they were good friends, they would let you do what you want and need to do."

"I know," he replied, rising. "Still and all, I can't be with you tonight. I'm going to go for a walk."

"Do you want company?" she asked.

He shook his head. "No. I need to walk alone."

"All right. Be safe, and I look forward to seeing you again soon, lover," she winked at him.

Callum gave her a weak smile back and then all but fled her apartment. He started walking the London streets, completely confused. What had gotten into him? Why had he left his perfectly willing mistress to walk out in the damp? It made no sense.

His feet took him right to the root of the problem, however. After about a half hour of walking, he found himself standing in front of Eleven Charles Place.

"Acton." Callum muttered the name as though it were a curse.

The curtains had not been drawn yet by whichever servant's job it was to draw them, and the man himself was sitting in the parlor with a hand over his face. Callum half expected to see he had been drinking, but there was nothing stronger in front of him than a cup of tea.

Without much thought about the hour, Callum walked up and knocked on the door.

Anne answered, blinking up at him in confusion. "Did you forget something here, your Grace?" she asked politely.

"I would like to speak with Sir Acton if he is available this evening," he replied stiffly.

"O-Of course, your Grace. I will announce you. But... if you intend to have words, might I ask that you keep your voices down? Her ladyship has retired for the evening," Anne said.

"I'll keep that in mind." He gave Anne a pointed look.

Anne opened the door so Callum could come into the foyer, then went to announce him to Sam.

She returned looking very concerned. "I'm not sure his lordship is in any fit state to receive, your Grace. I apologize."

"Oh? Tea a little too strong?" he countered.

"I'm afraid what's in the teacup stopped being tea a fair bit ago," she responded, much to Callum's surprise. "It might be best if you came back another time, your Grace."

"I'm afraid I must be rude and insist." He stared Anne down.

At first, the housekeeper drew herself up to her full diminutive height and stared right back at him. Then she wavered and gave in with a sigh. "Suit yourself."

He followed her into the parlor, where she leaned over Sam and gave him a careful shake. "Your lordship, his Grace, Duke Tennant, is here to see you."

Sam's brilliant blue eyes blinked open, albeit unfocused. He looked at Callum, then straightened himself up in his chair. "Tennant."

"Acton," he replied.

"What brings you here at this hour?" Sam picked up his teacup, stared into the bottom of it, then let Anne pry it out of his hand.

"I'll just bring you both some tea," she said pleasantly, and Callum had no doubt it was going to be very strong tea.

He took the chair next to Sam. "I came because I think I've been unfair to you. Hamilton pointed out to me that we all have secrets and, well, I've been keeping one from you. I thought, if I told you my secret, we could be more honest with each other."

Sam's eyes were bloodshot and bleary. Callum wondered how much he'd had to drink or, at his size, if he was even able to hold his liquor. Still, Sam managed to respond with force and clarity, "There are some things I cannot tell you. Not yet."

"Then tell me that. I would prefer that to a lie," he responded.

"If you are going to tell me a secret, I just want you to know there is only so much I can tell you in return," Sam said.

He nodded. "I understand. But I must tell you this before Hamilton comes haunting my nightmares. You see, I have a mistress."

Sam's face flashed displeasure before he could school it into something more neutral. "I know several men do."

"You disapprove," Callum went on.

"Only if you keep her if you marry my sister," he said.

"Ah. Then Hamilton was right," he grumbled. "You are not so understanding on that point."

"I assure you, Sabrina won't be, either," Sam replied firmly.

"That is good to know." He thanked Anne when she came back with the strongest tea Callum had ever tasted.

Sam sipped it and winced. "I'm not that far gone, Anne."

"So you say." She was completely unrepentant. "You gentlemen have a nice talk. And remember, her ladyship is sleeping."

"Thank you, Anne." Sam dismissed her.

Anne puttered around the room for a moment, drawing the shades and such. Then she gave Sam a hard look and left.

"How many people know your great secret that you cannot tell me?" Callum asked, getting the sense from Anne that she'd just given Sam a warning look.

"All of my staff. Most of the people I employ, here and at Acton," Sam said.

"And yet I would be one person too many?" he argued.

Sam sighed and sipped his tea. "No one in society knows."

"Except your sister."

"Except my sister."

"Not even Jeremy Acton, then?" Callum pressed.

Sam let out a bark of laughter at that. "He would be the very last person I would ever tell."

"But you will tell me if I marry Miss Sabrina?" he reiterated.

"I will."

"And if it is Hamilton who marries her?" he asked.

"I would still be more comfortable telling you than him, but I will have little choice in the matter. He will have to know if he marries Sabrina." Sam grimaced.

Callum set his cup down and leaned closer to him. "Either way, when Miss Sabrina is married, will you tell me?"

Sam looked thoughtfully at him for a while. Then he nodded. "When Sabrina is married, I will tell you."

A Walk in the Park

Theo

Callum was impeccably dressed, as usual, but his eyes had dark circles underneath them and were a bit bloodshot. Theo wondered how long he'd been out the night before with Mary.

"A bit obvious, aren't we?" Theo asked, frowning at his friend as the carriage stopped at Eleven Charles Place.

"Obvious?" Callum echoed.

"That you've been with your mistress. You'll have to confess to Acton now," he said.

To Theo's surprise, Callum chuckled. "I did. Last night."

"Pardon?" he replied, turning to fully face his friend.

"I didn't spend the night with Mary. I came here to see Acton. And trust me, he won't look to be in much better shape than I am," Callum said.

"Well, what did he say?" Theo asked.

His friend shrugged. "Let's just say he's more in your camp than mine on the subject."

Theo burst out laughing. "I knew it! I knew he'd never stand for it!"

"Yes, well, a broken clock is right twice a day, I suppose," Callum grumbled.

Theo was still laughing when the door to Eleven Charles Place opened. He jumped down before Callum could offer Sabrina a hand up into the carriage.

Sabrina looked beautiful, but a bit disgruntled today. Theo divined the reason when Sam came up behind her, smelling ever so slightly of cognac.

"I take it you overindulged last night?" Theo asked Sam.

Sam groaned and held his head. "I didn't think I did, but my head tells me differently."

Callum stifled a laugh. "That's because, after tea, we returned to cognac last night, if you remember."

"Don't remind me," Sam complained.

"Your Grace, this is *your* fault?!" Sabrina accused.

"Not so loud," Sam and Callum hissed together.

"Sam Acton, it is not like you to be taken in by such a bad influence," Sabrina scolded. Then the second shoe dropped. "Wait, what do you mean 'back' to cognac?"

Sam looked anywhere but at her.

"You didn't. You promised!" Sabrina folded her arms over her chest.

"I wasn't feeling well," Sam tried to defend himself.

"Oh, and you're feeling in the pink of health right now." She shook her head. "Honestly, Sam. And knowing we had an outing today besides!"

"I'm here, aren't I?" Sam grunted.

"Barely." She turned her attention to Callum. "And don't think I've forgotten about you."

Callum winced. "I wouldn't dream of such a thing."

"I am telling you just this once, Your Grace. Do *not* encourage my brother to drink! Do you understand me?!" Sabrina all but shouted.

Both Callum and Sam groaned again. "Yes, Miss Sabrina. I hear you," Callum said.

Theo listened to the entire exchange, biting back a smile. "And let this be a lesson to you," he added, a bit more loudly than he needed to.

Sam and Callum glowered at him.

"I think I am ready to go to the park now," Sabrina sniffed. "Whether these two are or not."

"Driver!" Theo called, making Sam and Callum grunt, "to Hyde Park!"

The carriage began bumping its way to the park.

"I am never drinking again," Sam said after two blocks of the rocking.

"I second that," Callum agreed.

"Good. I'm glad you've both learned your lesson." Sabrina turned to Theo. "Honestly, I'm beginning to doubt the duke is trying to court me at all."

"How terribly unfortunate that would be for me," Theo grinned.

Sabrina blushed and Theo's heart leapt. He wished Callum really was pulling out of the race. The man had been making far too much headway with the brother, and, much as it would behoove him to take this opportunity in the park to ingratiate himself with Sam, he wasn't about to miss the opportunity to walk side-by-side with Sabrina.

Callum and Sam would simply have to talk politics or some other such thing. Theo had no doubt they could entertain themselves.

When they reached Hyde Park, Theo directed the driver to take them to the north-west enclosure, near Kensington Gardens and the Serpentine River.

"It has the best views," Theo explained. He glanced at Sam. "And has not so suffocating a press of people as the main circle promenade."

Sam nodded his thanks while Sabrina simply stared out of the carriage in awe. "What a beautiful place this is! I am glad we didn't miss it."

Theo smiled indulgently while Callum and Sam continued to wince and nurse their hangovers every time Sabrina opened her mouth.

The carriage stopped at the north-west enclosure, and it was all Theo could do to get out of the carriage fast enough to catch Sabrina as she bounded from it in excitement.

"Sabrina," Sam said in a warning tone as Theo held on just a second too long.

Theo set her aside and offered her his arm. "There are many fine footpaths in this part of the park. And the gardens and the river, of course."

"Lead on, my friend," Callum responded, stepping down just before Sam.

With a soft smile, Sabrina put her hand on Theo's arm and they began to walk a path near the river.

Sam and Callum followed in their wake, again talking politics, this time about the classism of Hyde Park itself.

Sabrina looked up at Theo and sighed. "We are never to be free of politics."

"Does your brother not enjoy poetry?" he asked.

"Not nearly as much as he does history and politics. And other pursuits," Sabrina said.

"Other pursuits? Does your brother have a mistress, then?" Theo smiled.

Sabrina did not smile back. "He would never."

"Then you do not believe in mistresses." Theo delicately led her around a puddle.

"I do believe they exist, if that is what you're wondering. I do not believe a married man should have one," she sniffed.

Theo nodded. "My thoughts precisely."

"Though, it would seem His Grace is going to give his up, if we are to marry," Sabrina sighed. "Or so Sam tells it."

"I am convinced within myself that I will be the man marrying you, Miss Sabrina," Theo said seriously. "And therefore have eschewed mine already."

Sabrina stared at him. "You have a mistress?"

"Had," he corrected her. "I could tell in your voice when you talked of Sam not ever having a mistress that your true belief is that a man should not have one at all. But I believe it is important to be honest. Most men do take a mistress at one point or another, especially in their youth. But, like you, I do not believe in keeping one after marriage."

Theo braced himself for any sort of reaction.

She gave a sour pout. "I suppose she was a fine young woman of loose morals, and beautiful."

He raised an eyebrow at her. Jealousy? It took everything in him not to smile. "Her name is Angeline, and she is a fine young woman of loose morals, and beautiful. But she does not tempt my heart the way you do, and therefore, I could not, in good conscience, keep her."

Sabrina looked somewhat mollified. Then her eyes widened. "You did not cast her out on the streets, did you?!"

Theo did laugh at that. "I would never! I paid her expenses for at least three months, though I've no doubt she will find a new benefactor within a week. A man must take care of his responsibilities. I think it is reprehensible to leave one's mistress to starve, simply because you are no longer interested in seeing her."

"All right. That sounds... well, not ideal, but better," she said. "I do find the practice of mistresses distressing. I mean, a woman is not allowed to take a... I don't even know what you'd call it... a mister?"

"Many do after marriage. Most political marriages are not love matches, unfortunately. Often, the two do not suit each other well, and each takes their own lover or lovers outside of the marriage bed," he explained. "Though I would be most upset if you did so, as I'm sure you would be if I did."

"That is absolutely right," Sabrina replied primly. "Thankfully, my brother is allowing me to try to find a love match. I think I have already found him." She glanced at Theo with a blush. "But I cannot abide any mistresses."

The near-profession of love made Theo's heart soar. "Then we are in agreement," he said softly, trailing his fingertips over her hand.

The drone of political discourse abruptly stopped behind them.

"Hamilton!" Sam growled. "Just what do you think you're doing, taking liberties with my sister like that?"

"I was about to ask the same thing," Callum said, furious.

Theo snatched his hand back and took a step back from Sabrina. "Forgive me. I forgot myself, Miss Sabrina."

"I see no—" Sabrina began.

"Tennant, would you mind going ahead and escorting my sister while I have words with Hamilton, here?" Sam asked angrily.

"I would be delighted." Callum stepped forward and jabbed his arm in Sabrina's direction, more than offering it.

With a pained look at Theo, Sabrina took his arm and Callum began marching them ahead up the path.

"I hear duels are fought here, Hamilton." Sam wasted no time in threatening him. "I will have you know I am versed in all kinds. The sword. The pistol. I can even beat you to a bloody pulp if need be."

Theo held up his hands. "It was a moment I would take back if I could. I am sorry. I meant no insult to you or to your sister."

"You wouldn't take back the moment," Sam scoffed. "If I were not here, you would have kissed her or Lord only knows what else!"

He rubbed the back of his neck. "All right. Probably. Maybe a kiss. But I would not have done anything to besmirch her honor."

"Mhm. You are lucky she likes you and I cannot slaughter you in a duel," Sam continued.

"You think I am not also versed?" Theo raised an eyebrow.

"Are you saying you'd like to find out whether Eton or private tutelage are superior in the ways of battle?" he snapped.

Theo held up his hands again. "No. I forget myself again. I have no wish to die, and no wish to deprive Miss Sabrina of her brother, whichever way it would go."

"Then you will kindly keep your hands to yourself until after you are properly married, though you become less and less impressive in my eyes the longer I know you," Sam grunted.

"Give me a chance," Theo begged. "Please. Forget this incident. I am a good man, Acton, and the right man for your sister. I may not have the land, or the title, or the connections Tennant has, but I am not without means and I will use all of those means to make your sister happy."

Sam's jaw worked. "I have promised my sister I will give you a chance."

He relaxed. "Thank you."

"You will come to Acton within the month." Sam's tone brooked no objections.

"I will?" Theo blinked.

"With Tennant. Don't get too excited," he said. "I find London does not agree with my constitution, and have decided to remove myself back to Acton, which means I must bring Sabrina with me. Therefore, if the courtship is to continue, you will need to come to Acton."

"How long are you staying in town, then?" Theo asked.

"At most, I will bear another week. But, as you rudely informed me before, I have hurt my sister's chances in society beyond repair and there have been no further invitations. Therefore, if we are invited to no other social events within the week, we are leaving," Sam replied.

He nodded. "When you leave, I will follow. As I'm sure Tennant will."

Sam poked a finger in Theo's chest when he would have turned to go. "Do not disappoint me again, Hamilton."

"I won't," Theo promised.

Decorum

Sabrina

"You shouldn't have allowed that, you know," Callum said.

Sabrina expected it, but it still rubbed her the wrong way. "And what business is it of yours?"

"As one of your suitors, and potential husband, I believe it is very much my business," he replied. "You should never allow a man who is not your betrothed or your husband to touch you that way."

"You're only still one of my suitors because my brother likes you. Lord Hamilton eschewed his mistress right after meeting me. I believe you are hanging onto yours until marriage?" she said archly.

"Lord Hamilton has a big mouth." He frowned at Sabrina. "Or was it your brother telling tales?"

She drew herself up to her full height, only a few inches shorter than Callum. "My brother would never conceal something so important from me. And Lord Hamilton simply told me the facts of his case. He did not mention yours. I was angry that my brother had to explain such things to me as though I were a child. As if I do not know something of the world."

"You begrudge your brother a mistress, that I know for a fact," he said.

"I begrudge my brother nothing that would make him happy. He is simply too fine a man to sully a woman whose only choice in this world is to make a living on her back." Sabrina tugged her hand out of his arm and began hurrying ahead.

"Miss Sabrina, I am to escort you," he called in a warning tone.

"Then catch up," she snapped.

Callum hurried after her. "This is most unseemly."

"I am not enjoying my walk and would like to get it over with as soon as possible. My brother will, no doubt, scold me later as well. But as you are neither my brother nor my husband, I see no reason to carry on this conversation with you," Sabrina said.

He caught up to her and held out his arm once more, continuing at a brisk pace.

Reluctantly, she took it.

"I know you must have expected some manner of chastisement from me," he murmured. "So I must ask, what has you truly upset?"

"Men! Men have me upset," she lamented. "Don't you see? You can take whatever you wish, yet women have to beg for crumbs at your table. Taking advantage of women who need to debase them-selves in order to provide for themselves and their families—it's disgusting!"

"And you are quite sure your brother is not one of those same men?" he challenged.

Sabrina laughed. She ended up laughing so hard she had to stop and hold her side. "Oh, I am absolutely certain."

Callum raised an eyebrow. "I suppose you simply believe what he tells you."

"You've spoken with my brother on numerous occasions. Do you actually believe him to be keeping a mistress? At Acton?" she asked.

He pursed his lips. "No, I cannot say as I believe your brother would keep a mistress anywhere. But you do have a point about

Acton. Certainly you would know if he were keeping a mistress there."

"The servants talk. The workers talk. I can assure you, with absolute certainty, my brother is not keeping a mistress," she said.

"That makes me wonder several things about your brother that are not seemly to speak of in a lady's company," he muttered.

"Twigs and berries?" she teased.

Callum smiled. "Ah. There is the sense of humor I have grown to enjoy. I suppose that is one question. Another would be…"

"Has he ever been with a woman? No," she continued. "We are close enough to know that about each other. I have always told him I will tell him the truth if he tells me the truth."

"I suppose I may then ask, quite rudely, if you have been with a man? I preface this by saying it would not matter to me as much as you think if you had," he said.

"My brother has not been with a woman. I have not been with a man. There you have it," she responded.

"What do you do for entertainment at Acton?" he asked.

Sabrina laughed again. "Good Lord! So many things. We ride horses and dance on occasion. Read books. I play the pianoforte. Sam does some hunting and fishing, though he does allow me to come along on the fishing. He believes I should not familiarize myself with firearms."

"A wise choice. They are quite dangerous," he said.

"I do some drawing and watercolors as well. But those not as much." She shook her head. "If one lacks entertainment, it is not that there is not entertainment to be had, but that one lacks imagination."

Callum chuckled. "I do very much enjoy how opinionated you are."

"Yes, well, I'm a lady. I live to entertain," she said with a touch of sarcasm.

"I believe you live to take care of your brother. How ever will he survive at Acton without you?" he asked.

Her brows drew together. "I am not entirely certain. If he were not such an ass, I would ask Sam to give Acton over to cousin Jeremy and come live at my husband's estate with me. But I worry so over the servants and the workers. I do believe Jeremy would actually beat them."

"Your cousin is an ass," he agreed. "I would have your brother at my estate all the time. What does Hamilton think about such a proposition?"

"I haven't asked him," she admitted with a blush. "I guess I'm afraid to."

"At least you do not fear broaching such topics with me." Callum winked at her.

"Well, you are particularly infuriating," she said.

"It's a place to start."

They found themselves down by the river. "My brother has invited you to Acton, has he not?" she asked as they waited for the other two to catch up.

"He has. And if he hasn't threatened to kill Hamilton just now, I would assume he has extended the same invitation to him," he replied.

"Good. It will be better for all of us if we continue this at Acton," she said.

Callum glanced at her. "Better for Sam, you mean."

Her head came up. "That's very informal."

"It is. Are you going to tell on me?" he grinned.

She rolled her eyes. "I suppose, if you agree to stop scolding me over Lord Hamilton, I will not tell Sam you've used his given name without permission."

"Agreed."

Theo and Sam joined them then. As Theo did not look too worse for the wear, Sabrina assumed there had been no fisticuffs.

"No swords at dawn?" she teased Sam.

"Pistols," Sam replied with a face so serious Sabrina thought she might not be joking.

"He's joking," Theo said quickly. "I've actually been invited to Acton. Provided I do not bend the rules of decorum anymore."

Sam's warning look told Sabrina that Theo was not the only one who would be held to that standard if she wanted him to come to Acton. "I'm sure we can restrain ourselves," she sighed.

"I'm glad to hear it." Sam looked out over the water of the Serpentine River. "I've heard there's some trouble with people committing suicide here."

A flicker of panic went through Sabrina and she quickly took her sister's hand. "That is terrible."

"And terribly true. Percy Bysshe Shelley's wife, Harriet, took her life here," Callum confirmed.

"Well, none of us will be, and that's all we need to know about the subject." Sabrina tugged Sam away from the water by her good hand.

Callum, of course, missed nothing and Sabrina could just imagine the conversation he'd be having with her sister later.

"Are you having a hard day, Sam?" she whispered when they were just far enough away from the gentlemen.

"I just hurt a bit. I should not have indulged last night," Sam replied.

"Please don't go thinking of jumping in the river. I will be so lonesome without you. And evil Jeremy will get Acton and then where will everyone be?" Sabrina said.

Sam smiled at her and nodded. "Always the voice of reason."

"Except when it comes to displays of affection," she responded with a self-deprecating grin.

"Don't think you're going to get out of a good tongue-lashing about that." But Sam's mood had visibly improved and Sabrina decided the danger was over.

Theo and Callum rejoined them as they made their way back to the carriage. Callum was frowning at Sam with great concern and, for once, took the seat next to him, allowing Sabrina to sit next to Theo.

"I am very carefully keeping my hands to myself," Theo murmured to her as the carriage began to move. "If I am a very good boy, do you suppose your brother will allow us to stay for lunch?"

"I'm sure he will." But she turned to her sister anyway. "Sam? May our gentlemen friends stay for lunch?"

"I don't see why not," Sam said after a pause.

"And don't worry. I know I'm still getting a stern talking to later," Sabrina smiled.

Her sister chuckled and Callum looked a little less concerned.

They took the long way around London getting back to Eleven Charles Place. Theo pointed out all the sights to Sabrina while Sam smiled indulgently and Callum watched Sam.

If she didn't know any better, Sabrina would say Callum was sweet on her sister. But that wasn't how the world worked. Callum could not possibly know Sam was a woman, and men did not fall in love with other men. Did they?

Sabrina brushed the thought away. It was too strange to contemplate.

Once they did arrive at Eleven Charles Place, Callum allowed Theo to get out first and help Sabrina down.

Then Sam stepped out, followed by a protective Callum, who was still staring deep concern through the back of Sam's head.

"Lunch?" Sabrina asked brightly. "Anne, we have two guests for lunch. Please ask the cook to plan accordingly."

"Yes, your ladyship." Anne hurried off to do just that.

Sabrina got them all seated in the parlor, Theo and Callum in their usual chairs, Sabrina and Sam on the settee.

Anne popped her head into the parlor before any conversation could get started. "The cook says lunch will be ready in half an hour."

"Thank you, Anne," Sabrina said. "It was a lovely day at the park—"

"Pardon the interruption, Miss Sabrina, but I would beg your indulgence. Might you call Anne back in here to chaperone yourself and Hamilton here? I would like to speak to Acton privately in his study," Callum interjected.

Sabrina bit her lip. It was as she had feared. "I..."

"If you think you're brokering marriage, Tennant," Theo warned.

Callum shook his head. "No. Another matter. I swear on my honor."

"This is quite abrupt," Sam frowned.

Callum dragged him up by the arm. "It cannot wait."

"I don't know of a topic we could discuss that cannot be discussed in front of my sister," Sam said.

"I know. But I also know it is a topic you would not wish to discuss in front of Hamilton." Callum gave Sam a long, hard look.

"I don't understand," Theo responded. "What's going on?"

Sabrina sighed and called for Anne. "Go. But please, be delicate."

Callum nodded and marched Sam out of the parlor.

"Miss Sabrina, what...?" Theo asked.

"His Grace saw something at the park I wish he had not. And that is all you need to know about the subject for now," she said quickly. "Now, shall we discuss lighter topics?"

Theo frowned, but finally nodded. "Yes."

Rivers and Burns

Sam

"What is this about, Tennant? You're acting quite strangely," Sam said once they were in her study.

Callum closed the door. "Are you suicidal?"

Sam stared at him. "Pardon?"

"You heard me. Have you tried to kill yourself?" he demanded.

"I would... I would hardly call this an appropriate conversation," Sam evaded.

"I'm taking that as a 'yes.'" He sounded furious. "How could you do something so selfish? To your sister, especially! What sort of prospects would you expect her to have without you? Without Acton? If you were placed in an asylum? A pig farmer, perhaps?"

Sam squared her shoulders. "First, Tennant, it is none of your business. Second, your concern for my well-being is touching, but I assure you there is nothing for you to worry about. I would never leave my sister to fend for herself."

"And when your sister marries?" Callum demanded.

She set her jaw, but ended up looking away from his piercing gaze. "There is still Acton to think of."

"Oh, I'm sure you've already thought of that. A man as smart as you." Callum moved to stand over her, the few inches he had on her. "Out with it. What is your plan for Acton?"

"I'm sure I don't know what you—"

He grabbed her by the collar. "Don't lie to me."

Sam swallowed. "As I have said, I am leaving Acton to one of my sister's sons."

"But in the meantime?" he asked.

"I... haven't decided yet. Acton practically runs itself. You and Hamilton would not find it a burden," she said.

"And in the past? Why was Miss Sabrina so worried about you at the park today?" he continued.

She turned her face away. "I would rather not discuss this, Tennant."

Callum ran his fingertip down the scar that seared up her neck and behind her ear and she began to struggle in his grip. "Let me go!"

"You think *this* is any reason to deprive this world of your presence?!" he shouted.

"I think it is none of your affair, now let me go!" She gave him a hard shove.

"At Eton, there was a boy very much like you. He was a sensitive creature, and felt deeply about his causes." He let go of her collar and shook his head. "He was tormented mercilessly by the other boys, and he couldn't handle it. He was a friend. I wish he'd come to me. You are too important, do you understand me? You are too important to your sister, to Acton, hell, to me!"

"To you?" Her brow furrowed.

"You don't even know what a rare person you are." He shook his head. "You mustn't hurt yourself. If you are lonely, come to Conford. Even if you don't choose me for your sister, come to Conford. I mean it."

"Why?" she asked. "I don't understand."

Callum grabbed Sam by the shirtfront and pressed his lips to hers.

At first, she was startled. Then she melted without thinking.

When he pulled away, she was dazed.

"I'm sorry," he stuttered. "I—"

Not knowing how else to respond, Sam punched him with a mean right hook.

He stumbled back, his lip split. It quickly began to bleed.

"What in the name of all that is holy, Tennant?!" Sam bellowed, wiping at her mouth.

"I'm sorry. I'm sorry. I don't know what came over me. I'm—"

"Yes, I heard. You're sorry." She took another step backward. "I think you need to leave."

Callum looked stricken. "Please, don't let this ruin our friendship. I was out of my mind, thinking of you trying to kill yourself. I don't know what happened."

She closed her eyes. "I am willing to forget this incident ever happened, but I am going to need at least this afternoon to make that happen."

"All right. I'll go for now." He shakily straightened his clothing and dabbed his lip with a handkerchief. "Will you tell your sister?"

"Absolutely not. She doesn't know that... such desires are possible," she said.

"Right. Yes. Of course. Thank you." He turned for the door of the study. "I am sorry, Acton."

"We will discuss this matter at a later date. For now, please collect Hamilton and go. I know you have an agreement that one cannot be present without the other while courting my sister," she replied.

Callum walked stiffly out the door.

Sam, shaking, went to sit behind her desk. She touched her lips, unable to believe what had just happened.

Scant minutes later, Sabrina came bustling in. "Sam, are you all right? I saw His Grace's face. What happened?"

"You wouldn't believe me if I told you. And I told him I would not tell you, and I intend to keep my word. Suffice it to say, he crossed a boundary," she replied.

Sabrina approached the desk. "Your clothes are all rumpled. Did you fight?"

"Yes. We fought. I won. Let us leave it at that," Sam said.

"What were you talking about?" Sabrina pressed.

She gave her sister a warning look. "I said we won't be discussing that."

"Fine." Sabrina settled herself in the chair across the desk from Sam. "I'm just curious about what had you so upset that you needed to punch him. And spoil lunch."

"Ah, there we come to the real problem. I spoiled your lunch with Hamilton," Sam said bitterly.

"I think Duke Tennant came in here to question you about things you've done in the past. Involving bodies of water," Sabrina countered. "And I think you punched him because of it."

"Think what you like." Sam pulled some correspondence out and began to go through it. He grimaced. "It appears we are not so unpopular as I thought. We have received one invitation to another ball."

Sabrina tsked. "Don't look so happy about it."

"I'm not. Why should I be happy? As Tennant said, we have a perfectly good pair of suitors now. I don't see why we need to go adding others," she grumbled.

"That's a change of tune for you. What happened to wanting me to have the pick of the lot?" Sabrina asked.

"I don't want to invite a whole hoard of suitors to Acton," Sam sighed, massaging the bridge of her nose.

"You could just let me have the one I want," her sister suggested.

"We'll see." Sam looked up at Sabrina, raising her eyebrow. "Are we finished here? I need to write some letters. Acton does not run itself."

Sabrina stood, but argued, "Of course it does. That's the way you have it set up."

"All right. Then would you mind leaving me in peace?" Sam asked testily.

She gathered up her skirts. "Sometimes, I don't understand you at all, *Samantha* Acton." She flounced out of the study.

Sam thought for a long moment, then pulled a piece of blank paper in front of her and dipped her pen in the ink well.

To His Grace Callum Tennant, Duke of Conford,

Regarding the incident that occurred today at Eleven Charles Place.

I am reminded of the Greeks and Romans, and can only attribute what happened to a deep friendship based on mutual idealism.

That being said, we do not live in Ancient Greece or Rome. I am sorry for what part I played in the incident, and I am also sorry for punching you afterward. My only excuse is that I was startled.

I hope we may put this incident behind us and continue our friendship. I must say it has enriched my life thus far and I would fain lose it.

Also, apparently we will be at the Thomas's Ball. I hope to see you there.

Sir Samuel Acton, Baronet of Acton

Sam looked down at the letter she had just written. Her lips still tingled from the unexpected kiss. She reached up to touch them, then balled her hand into a fist.

"There is no point in developing impossible notions at this juncture. You are too old for such foolishness," she said aloud of all of her eighteen years.

She rang for the steward and handed him the letter addressed to Callum. "Do please make sure this reaches him as soon as possible."

"Of course, your lordship," the steward replied.

Once he left, Sam sat back down in her chair. At least it could be said that Callum was passionate, she supposed. It was a trait she was sure her sister wanted in a man.

He likely saw Sabrina when he looked at her.

"Yes, that must be it," she decided. But then she remembered him running his fingers over her scars and frowned. She touched the scars that ran up behind her ear.

Sabrina stuck her head in again after a few hours. "It is time for dinner, Sam. And you are still looking very perplexed. Why will you not tell me what happened? Do you think it will affect my thoughts on Duke Tennant?"

"Possibly. But I promised. You understand what that means, of course," Sam said.

"Yes. I wish you would be forthright with me if you think Duke Tennant has done something I would find indefensible," her sister sighed. "I know you, Sam. I know you don't just go around punching people because they annoy you. Something drastic must have happened."

"And I will still keep my promise," she replied stiffly.

Sabrina groaned. "You are impossible. And stubborn. Impossibly stubborn."

"You like that about me." Sam rose. "Shall we go to dinner?"

"Yes," Sabrina said, hooking her arm through her sister's. "Let's."

One Ball too Many

Theo

The Thomas's Ball was much smaller than the Barrington's Ball, which may have accounted for the fact that the Actons received an invitation. Theo wasn't complaining. He was glad, after whatever had happened the afternoon before, Sam hadn't fled back to his estate and taken his sister with him. Sabrina deserved to savor all the delights of London. Having her go home before she'd had the opportunity to do so would have been a terrible shame.

Callum was looking nervous, a state Theo's friend did not usually occupy. When Sam showed up with Sabrina on his arm, he looked infinitely relieved and strode forward to say his hellos, Theo right behind him.

"Might I be first on your dance card, Miss Sabrina?" Theo asked when Callum and Sam just stared at each other. Callum was still sporting a cut lip, but some sort of mutual agreement must have passed between them because, after a few moments, both men just smiled.

"If you are first, then I shall be last. And I demand two dances," Callum interrupted.

Sabrina shook her head in good humor and offered up her dance card. "There you go, gentlemen. My dance card is wide open for you."

"Pity it will remain so," Jeremy sniped, walking up to them. "What a terrible scandal for you to show up at this ball, Sam."

"I thought we agreed to not be related for the rest of our time in London," Sam replied while Theo and Callum both scowled at Jeremy.

"We did. But poor Sabrina must need someone to fill up her dance card. I thought I'd take pity on her and put my own name down," he said.

"They were invited, Acton. Were you?" Theo asked.

Jeremy raised his chin. "Why, of course I was. Perhaps they thought there would be a lack of entertainment for the evening and decided to invite the most scandalous people they could think of."

"Ah. That's how you made the list," Callum retorted.

"I think the scandal is all on you, Jeremy. You're the one spreading such vulgar rumors," Sam said.

When Jeremy went to put his name on Sabrina's dance card, she snatched it back. "There is nothing on this earth that would induce me to spend a dance with you, Jeremy Acton. Now please, move along. You are ruining our evening."

Jeremy's eyebrows shot up. "Why, I never," he groused, insulted. He turned on his heel and stalked off.

"I'm sure that's going to turn into something blown out of proportion," Callum sighed.

"There is no winning with him, regardless," Sam said. "I'd rather he keep his filthy hands off my sister. I'm sure he wouldn't mind if the both of you ended your courtships, allowing him to swoop in and offer himself as a suitor."

Sabrina paled. "You would not consider such a thing."

"My dear sister, I am afraid you will end up a spinster before I will ever offer your hand to Jeremy Acton," Sam responded firmly.

"Good." Sabrina smiled at Theo. "I believe I do hear the first dance striking up."

Theo grinned back. "I believe I do as well." He offered Sabrina his arm.

Sabrina went with him out onto the dance floor, glancing behind just once at Sam and Callum.

"Don't worry. Men throw a punch at each other at least once during their friendship. It just shows how great of friends they are," Theo reassured her.

"Sam will not say a word about what transpired between them." She huffed. "It is quite vexing. Sam usually has such good manners. I'm afraid he does not want to tell me something that will color my view of Duke Tennant."

He considered for a moment, glancing back at Callum. "I do know what transpired, and I do think it would affect your view of him. But it would be from a lack of understanding, not because of any wrongdoing on anyone's part. They have forgiven each other. That is enough."

"Speaking of lack of understanding, you've just confused me more," she muttered.

"It is really something quite trivial for a student of history. Acton put Callum in his place, and that is all there is to it." Theo knew he was only fueling Sabrina's curiosity, but he did want her to feel the subject had been properly put to rest.

"You men and your secrets." She looked disappointed.

It pulled at his heartstrings. "I promise, once we are married, I will explain everything."

"But what if Sam chooses Duke Tennant?" she asked worriedly. "I don't want it to happen, but Sam does seem to like him better."

"You think your brother would choose Tennant over your objections?" he responded, fear also creeping into him. It had never occurred to him that Sam would choose against Sabrina's wishes.

Sabrina shrugged helplessly. "I don't know. I have told him over and over that I want you, but he continues to insist on giving Duke

Tennant a chance. You are both invited to Acton, after all. I can only assume he's hoping I'll make a different choice."

"I haven't made a very good impression on him, I will admit." Theo felt stricken. "I should try harder."

"If you will leave the scarring be, it would be a good start," she scolded him gently.

"We'll have to away to Gretna Green otherwise," he laughed.

She rolled her eyes. "We are not quite there yet, my Lord Hamilton."

Theo felt a bump at his back and turned to see Jeremy dancing with a plain girl who was far too young for him. He did not like the smile Jeremy gave him.

"Pardon me," Jeremy said. "I could not help but overhear. Do you intend to spirit my cousin away to Gretna Green?"

"It was said in jest, Jeremy," Sabrina angrily insisted. "And do you never attend to your own affairs? Are you too busy bringing misery to the lives of others?"

"One must have some form of entertainment." He grinned at them. "Have a lovely evening." He danced away with the girl who could be no more than fifteen.

"Why do I always get a bad feeling every time I encounter him?" Theo asked.

"Because he's going right now to tell the entirety of society that I am going to elope with you to Gretna Green." Sabrina's face was pale with both anger and fear. "We must go to Sam and Duke Tennant. There is no telling what will happen if the rumor reaches them before we do."

Theo stopped dancing abruptly and hurried as fast as he could without causing a stir back to Sam and Callum, Sabrina on his arm.

"What's wrong?" Sam asked. "Sabrina, did you twist an ankle?"

"Cousin Jeremy is about to cause trouble again," she sighed, catching her breath. "He overheard Lord Hamilton joking with me over going to Gretna Green..."

Callum looked at Theo. "Do you never think before opening your mouth?"

"I didn't know he was standing right behind me," he replied. "He is a conniving snake of a man."

Sam squeezed his eyes shut. "First, you will never be going to Gretna Green. I forbid it. Second, I am sure Jeremy is spreading the rumor like wildfire. Third, I have a feeling we will be leaving this ball in much the same manner as we did the last one—in a cloud of societal shame."

"It was just a joke, Sam. Even Jeremy knew it. He's being viscous on purpose," she pleaded. "Please don't think less of Lord Hamilton."

"It is disconcerting how often you need to repeat that phrase," Sam grunted. But he gave in with a sigh. "I can hardly hold anything Jeremy does against friends. He is an odious toad, and if he had not settled upon your little jest, he would have found something else to besmirch our good name. Again."

Theo found it heartening that Sam at least referred to him as a friend. "Are you sure you don't wish one of us to challenge him to a duel?"

"He's too much a coward to accept," Callum snorted.

"That is true. And he is tiptoeing right at the line of insult, not quite crossing it far enough to warrant a duel. He has not questioned either of our honor. Just my manhood and your judgment," Sam said.

Fans were up all around, heads pressing together as Jeremy circulated around the room. Theo wanted to wring the bastard's neck.

Soon, the hostess, Lady Thomas approached.

"Gentlemen, I do hate to interrupt, but I'm afraid I must ask Sir Acton and Miss Acton to leave," she said primly.

"Here we go," Sam grumbled.

"It is no fault of yours, of course, Sir Acton. I simply cannot have a woman who would so casually mention Gretna Green around other young ladies of breeding. There is nothing the matter with you," Lady Thomas added, though her gaze did flick to the front of Sam's pants.

Theo put a hand on Sam's shoulder. "It is I who must leave, then, Lady Thomas, for I was the one who suggested Gretna Green. In jest, but there you have it. Miss Sabrina said not a word about it."

"And I believe Sir Acton's face is a bit higher, if you are being polite, Lady Thomas," Callum said icily.

Lady Thomas's cheeks flushed. "I meant no disrespect."

"We will leave, of course, Lady Thomas. I can see you prefer the company of the Jeremy Acton sort to people of good manners. I, for one, will accept no further invitations from Farwell House." Callum offered his arm to Sabrina, who took it graciously.

Theo walked side-by-side with Sam behind the pair while Lady Thomas was still stuttering her apologies.

Once out in the open air, Sam relieved Callum of Sabrina. "It was nice to see you gentlemen this evening, despite the outcome," he said.

"You will be returning to Acton," Callum assumed.

"Tomorrow, yes. I expect you will come to visit us within a fortnight?" Sam asked.

"Tomorrow?" Sabrina and Theo protested together.

"Surely not, Acton," Theo said. "Miss Sabrina has barely had time to take in the sights!"

"I am sure, once she is married, Sabrina will spend many an enjoyable month here," Sam replied. "Unfortunately, I do not have the fortitude to continue to deal with Jeremy's backstabbing, and I know, after tonight, there will be no more invitations."

Theo bowed his head. "I am sorry, Acton. That is my fault."

"Not at all. As I said, Jeremy would have settled on some excuse or another to spread more rumors about us. I simply cannot abide rumors being spread about Sabrina. I'm sure I could endure another week, if it weren't for the lies being spread about my sister. It is better I take her home," Sam said. "And entertain only those two men who have stood by us regardless."

"I am honored by your invitation, and we will certainly find our way to Acton within a fortnight," Theo responded.

"I am honored as well, and see no impediment to our arrival at Acton within a fortnight," Callum added.

Sabrina looked disappointed. "Sam, you will never return here. I had so hoped you might find some enjoyable pastime while you were here. But it has been nothing but a nuisance to you and I feel badly about that."

Sam patted her hand. "It will be a relief to return home. I simply am not meant for big cities, that is all. A good country living will always see me right."

"Come to the club with us tonight," Theo suggested.

The other three turned to stare at him.

Theo felt the back of his neck heat up. "That is to say, you should enjoy that once, at least, before returning to Acton. No mistresses or anything like that. Just good times, good cigars, good cognac—"

"No cognac," Sabrina and Callum said together.

"All right, no cognac. But cards and just good camaraderie with other men of your station. I understand you do not entertain, nor do you go to many local functions. You should have a little gentlemanly fun while you are still in London. Just tonight. In the morning, you may return to Acton, as you plan to. Tonight, spend some time with Tennant and me," Theo continued.

Sam's eyebrows drew together and he looked at Sabrina.

"You should go, Sam. I will retire for the evening and make sure to have an early start tomorrow to see that we are packed and on our way," Sabrina said.

With a swallow, Sam turned to the other two men. "All right."

The Club

Callum

Sam seemed awfully nervous, but Callum thought he understood. Far from being a country bumpkin, Sam was like one of those geniuses who functioned best in isolation, quietly improving the world while not being entirely of the world.

Theo talked on and on about the club as they made their way there, extolling its many wonderful virtues, though skipping the part about the mistresses. It wasn't as though the club were laden with them, anyway. There were far more men in the club just happy to enjoy some time away from their domestic life than there were men with mistresses on their arms.

With an inner chuckle, Callum recalled that he and Theo had recently been two of those men. It was good they were going tonight, though. He hoped Mary would be there so he could break it off properly. While it was entirely possible—even probable—that Theo would win Sabrina, something about how Sam explained his feelings on a man who was serious about a domestic life struck a chord in Callum. If another woman of quality like Sabrina entered his orbit, he did not want a mistress hanging over their courtship that would potentially disappoint good brother-in-laws like Sam.

When the cigar smoke rolled out of the club as the door opened, Sam coughed.

Theo's eyes widened immediately. "I'm sorry, Acton. Are you sensitive to smoke?"

He had gained a modicum of intelligence over the subject and did not ask if it was because of Sam's injuries.

"A bit. But it hasn't stopped me from enjoying one or two good cigars," Sam replied, trying to get into the spirit of things.

"How many? One or two?" Callum teased him.

Sam's cheeks colored. "Two."

"Good God, man! And in the country, too, where there was likely none of quality! Oh, we must fix that," Theo insisted.

The doorman barely blinked an eye at us as we entered. "Your usual table, gentlemen?"

"Yes. And for our guest, Sir Samuel Acton, Baronet of Acton," Theo said.

The doorman's eyes flicked up, then. "Sir Acton?"

If the doorman glanced down at Sam's privates, Callum was sure he'd be the one punching someone today.

"Pardon me. I've just heard so much about you from my fiancee. She's a servant in the Acton household," the doorman went on in a rush. "She says what a good, fair employer you are."

"Oh dear, Rick, are we losing you to the Acton Estate?" Theo laughed and Callum's hackles went down.

"Not at all. Jenny, isn't it? Yes, she did say she would be moving to London within a month. We will all be sad to see her go. She is an excellent maid. I would recommend her anywhere," Sam replied with a warm smile.

Callum supposed this small connection to Acton put Sam a little more at ease. Then he remembered that Sam's staff knew a certain secret about him. He made the connection in his head when Rick gave Sam a sympathetic look that likely it was that the staff knew Sam had been suicidal once or twice in his day.

"You're a good man, Sir Acton. A great one. We're both grateful for your recommendation," Rick said.

"It's the least I can do for Jenny after the good care she's taken of us all these years." Sam seemed a little less comfortable. "Of course, there are some things that must stay at Acton…"

"Absolutely, Sir Acton," Rick responded quickly. "I just never thought I'd have the privilege of meeting you in person. Please, enjoy your evening. Dennis will take you to your table. Dennis?"

Dennis had quietly shown up sometime during the conversation. He very professionally led us to our usual table and we sat down.

"Our usual cigars, Dennis. But no cognac tonight, thank you," Callum said.

Dennis looked surprised for just a moment before his professional demeanor returned. "Of course, Your Grace."

"Shall we play Hazard?" Theo asked. "Or would you prefer cards?"

"Acton, do you play cards? I mean, other than the usual parlor kind." Callum looked over at Sam, and had to hide a smile when he saw a twinkle in Sam's eye.

"I have been known to play Vingt-et-un with Sabrina," Sam said.

Both men stared at him. "You taught your sister how to play Vingt-et-un?" Theo gaped.

"She taught me, actually. I still don't know how she learned it. I finally learned to best her, most of the time. She is a terrible liar, but she has the devil's luck. She'd make an awful cheat," Sam responded.

"We must play, then. I don't suppose you've played for money?" Theo asked.

"My sister and I have our wagers. But nothing as high stakes as I'm sure we'll be playing for tonight," Sam challenged.

"Oh-ho! You intend to win, do you?" Theo laughed.

Sam just nodded with a secretive smile. "I always play to win."

Callum asked Dennis to bring a deck of cards when he returned with their cigars.

To Sam's credit, he did a manful job of puffing away at a cigar, but Theo and Callum could both tell it was not to his liking.

Callum finally plucked the cigar away. "I'll not waste a good cigar on a man who can't appreciate it."

Sam laughed. "Well, I tried."

Theo shuffled the deck. "Face cards are worth ten, numbered cards face value, Aces are eleven or one, player's choice."

"Yes, we've all played Vingt-et-un," Callum said.

"I just want to make sure Acton here knows the house rules. Knock when you think you're closest to twenty-one, but lose that turn. You're playing against the dealer. If the dealer has twenty-one or is the closest to twenty-one without going bust, the dealer wins. If the dealer goes bust or you have more than the dealer without going over, you win." Theo began to deal.

"Mighty confident, taking the dealer place first," Sam observed, flicking his bottom card up to look at it and then tapping the table for another, as he was in the elder spot.

"I'm quite confident I can beat both of you," Theo grinned.

"What shall we say the stakes are?" Callum asked.

"Well, I'm certainly not wagering Acton. I'm afraid Jeremy will show up to play," Sam joked.

The other two men laughed.

"It is a friendly game. Perhaps a pound a stake?" Theo said.

"I think that sounds just fine," Sam replied.

They played several rounds before Callum had to stop Theo from playing another because they were losing quite embarrassing amounts of money to Sam.

"And you say your sister has the devil's luck," Theo complained as Callum handed the cards back to Dennis. "Now I'm terrified to play her at Quadrille!"

"Who says she plays Quadrille?" Sam chuckled. "When she is so good at Vingt-et-un."

Callum and Theo groaned. "We shall lose our estates to those two," Callum said.

"No doubt," Theo agreed.

They were sharing a good laugh over that when two men came trudging over, a third bolstered up between them. The third was a young gentleman, probably in his first year of being allowed in a club, and he was completely drunk. He blinked over at their table and pointed. "Heyyy, twig and berries!"

That would have been fine with Callum, except that his companions started to laugh, as did other gentlemen at nearby tables.

"Tennant?" Sam asked as Callum stood.

"I've had quite enough of that," Callum said, getting right up in the drunkard's face.

"Why not show us, then? Put the rumors to rest," one of his companions suggested with a smirk. "Hell, we can all take bets! Twig and berries, no twig and berries."

Callum smiled tightly at the man. Then he cocked his fist back and punched him so hard he stumbled back, dropping his friend.

"Tennant!" Theo and Sam exclaimed together, standing.

The man Callum had punched held his bleeding nose. "You bastard! You're going to regret that." He came at Callum.

Theo and Sam jumped in to help their friend, while the other man completely dropped the drunkard to wade into the fray with the man with the bloody nose. The young drunk gentleman flopped to the floor with a thump.

"Gentlemen, please!" Rick and Dennis, along with other staff came to try to break things up, even as other gentlemen were beginning to bet on which side would win.

"They're all getting black-balled," one man snorted from behind his paper.

"I'll take stakes on that," another man said from a nearby table.

"You can't take stakes on that. All you'd have to do is put in a black ball and then you'd win," his friend told him.

"Hmm. True."

Shouts of bets, rising higher and higher as the drunkard weaved his way off the floor, rang out around them as fists flew among the six men. Soon, it became apparent that, though as a group they were not as young as the men who'd accosted them, Callum, Theo, and Sam were going to win.

In fact, Sam threw one last punch, and the third man hit the floor, holding his jaw.

"I think you broke his jaw!" the bloody-nosed young man griped at Sam.

"Maybe next time the only twig and berries he concerns himself with will be his own," Callum said.

"Someone send for the doctor!" the bloody-nosed man called, and Rick nodded to Dennis, who ran out of the establishment.

Everyone thought the fight was over, and went back to the conversations they'd been having before, shelling out money to those who had won the wager, and the winners crowing over their winnings.

Sam turned his back to return to the table, and the drunkard got it into his head to pick up a bottle.

Before Theo and Callum could react, the drunkard broke the bottle over the back of Sam's head. Sam went down hard.

"Acton!" Callum knelt down, feeling for a pulse while Theo made the drunkard regret his poor decision.

Sam was unconscious, but breathing.

"Loosen his collar, get the man some air!" Callum started undoing Sam's cravat.

"I'll take care of him, sir," Rick said, interceding quickly. Callum didn't have time to argue before Rick bodily lifted Sam in his arms. He carried Sam upstairs to an empty gentleman's quarters, Callum and Theo right on his tail.

"Please, gentlemen, send the doctor up here as soon as he arrives. You need not linger." Rick began shooing Callum and Theo to the doorway.

"He's our friend," Callum argued.

"Yes, and he needs a doctor. Please, go wait for him," Rick responded.

Stymied by Rick, then two other staff, Theo and Callum had no choice but to return to the main hall and wait for the doctor.

"Someone should tell his sister," Callum said to Theo.

"You won't leave him to do it yourself, will you?" he replied.

Callum let out a long sigh. "No."

Theo nodded. "I think you and Acton need to have a long talk when this is all settled. And I don't think Miss Sabrina will put up with what you may be thinking about Greece and Rome."

"I know." Callum rubbed the back of his neck. "Still and all, I cannot leave him."

"I'll go tell Miss Sabrina." Theo clapped Callum on the shoulder. He passed the drunkard and scowled at him.

"Don't worry, Hamilton. I have no doubt Lord Hampton will be blackballed in every club in London by the end of the week." Dennis, returning with the doctor, said.

The two friends of the drunkard began to loudly complain about their nose and jaw, but Dennis ushered him right past them without so much as a look in their direction, and headed for the stairs.

Callum started after them, but was blocked by Rick himself from entering Sam's room. "Privacy, Your Grace," Rick said by way of excuse.

Indeed, within moments, the doctor ordered for the door to be closed, admitting only himself and Rick.

With nothing else to do, Callum paced in front of the door, worrying if his friend had suffered a brain injury.

And wondering why the hell they wouldn't let him in.

A Little Accident

Theo

The carriage had barely stopped in front of Eleven Charles Place before Theo jumped out. Anne met him at the door, looking rather disgruntled.

"Please, Anne, can you wake Miss Sabrina?" Theo asked.

She blinked away her sour demeanor and it was replaced with concern. "Where is his lordship?"

"There's been an accident. He's at the club, but with a doctor—" he began.

She turned, her skirt bunched in her fist as she took the stairs two at a time. "Your ladyship!" she called loudly.

Not entirely sure what to do as he'd been left on the doorstep, Theo decided it was probably best he let himself in and close the door before the whole neighborhood heard Anne yelling.

He waited patiently in the foyer, idly going through the dish of calling cards, but there were still only his and Callum's within it. That gave him a sense of relief. It was hard enough competing with just his best friend.

There was a rustle several minutes later and he looked up to see a hastily-dressed Sabrina hurtling herself down the stairs.

She was in such a hurry that she tripped on the third stair from the bottom.

Theo stepped in to catch her, the feel of her against him distracting him momentarily. "I don't know if they'll let you in the club..."

"They will let me in," Sabrina replied in a tone that would scare a lesser man.

"I asked the carriage to wait," he said. "Are you ready to go?"

"Yes. Take me to him," she responded. "And on our way, tell me what happened."

He nodded and escorted her out to the carriage. Anne came as well for decorum's sake. She settled in next to her mistress with a carpet bag.

"What are you bringing?" he asked.

"Never you mind," Anne snapped and he decided it would be best not to bother the woman. She might be a servant, but clearly, in this crisis, she'd taken over the role of matron.

"Some clothes for Sam," Sabrina answered with a sigh. "Anne, you don't need to bite his head off. I'm sure he had nothing to do with whatever happened."

Theo rubbed the back of his neck.

Both women narrowed their eyes on him. "What happened?" Sabrina asked.

"In fairness, they started it. These young pups with their drunk friend started laughing over... well... twigs and berries..." he said.

"You ended up in fisticuffs," Sabrina concluded.

He nodded. "But the fight had ended and we had won. The drunkard was sore over it and grabbed a bottle and smashed it over the back of Acton's head."

"That louse!" Anne exclaimed.

"That was our thoughts exactly," he replied. "He's with a doctor now. He was knocked right out."

"I hope he's all right," Sabrina fretted.

"I'll make sure he is, your ladyship," Anne said.

The carriage stopped a few minutes later in front of the club, and Theo was just fast enough to jump out and help Sabrina down. He helped Anne as well.

"Aren't you the gentleman," Anne smiled. Then she was all business once more and hurried Sabrina to the club door.

Theo recognized Dennis and quickly caught up to the women. "This is Miss Sabrina Acton, Sir Acton's sister, and her maid. Would it be possible to let us in?"

"I'll have to check with Mr. Watts, sir." Dennis said. "But I'll be quick." He left his post to another servant and quickly dashed upstairs.

Callum came down with Dennis a few minutes later. "The doctor said he will admit the two women, but no one else," Callum grunted, frustrated.

"We can't go in? Still?" Theo asked.

"No. Apparently not."

Theo made a face. "That's downright rude."

"I'm sure Sam appreciates your concern, but he is a very private man. And his... scarring will likely be exposed," Sabrina explained quietly.

"Oh," both men said together, realization dawning.

"Yes, so have a cognac, blackball that louse, and let us get to it," Anne sniffed, taking Sabrina's arm and starting to pull her toward the stairs.

"We should put it to a vote," Callum observed, looking at Dennis.

Dennis shrugged. "When Mr. Watts is back, I'll ask him. Likely, he'll talk to the owner and we'll have the vote as soon as tomorrow. But you should know, you two will also be up for consideration."

"We understand," Theo said while Callum looked affronted.

"That man had no business—"

"We understand," Theo reiterated, giving Callum a hard look.

Callum sighed and nodded. "Thank you, Dennis, for all you're doing."

"It's my pleasure," Dennis said. "And, Your Grace, my Lord, it is my fervent hope that neither of you are blackballed. It is always a delight to have you here."

The two men nodded and went back to their regular table. Each nursed a snifter of cognac, not really drinking, as they worried about their friend.

"How was Miss Sabrina?" Callum asked.

"Terrified, I'm sure, but determined. You should have seen the maid, though. I thought for sure she was going to murder me where I stood," Theo replied.

"Anne? Yes, I did get the sense she could be truly terrifying." He nodded.

"Well, she is." Theo swirled cognac around in his snifter, then put it back down on the table without taking a drink.

Callum did the same. "What was in the bag?"

"Miss Sabrina said it was a change of clothes for Acton, but Anne was quite a bit more cagey about it," Theo said. "In truth, I'm not sure."

"It probably is just clothes," his friend responded. But Theo could tell he didn't believe it.

"What do you think it is?" Theo asked.

"Money," Callum said. "Though for what, I can't be certain."

"For the doctor, most likely. I don't know why they'd hide that fact, though," Theo mused.

"I don't, either."

Paying the Price

Sabrina

"I take it you know *your sister* is not what she appears to be?" the doctor said once the door closed behind Sabrina and Anne.

Rick was standing in a corner, guarding the door and keeping a weather eye on the entire situation. "Sir Acton is just doing what's best for everyone, doctor. There's no need for any fuss," he interrupted before Sabrina could say anything.

"What's best for everyone?" the doctor echoed.

"As you can see, my sister is unmarriable. If she did not pretend to be Sir Acton, the estate of Acton would go to my cousin Jeremy," Sabrina began.

"Horrible, heartless man," Anne said.

"And we would be at his mercy. It was our father's idea, after the fire that burned her and took our stepmother," Sabrina continued. "Sam has been raised entirely as a man, though, of course, she knows she is a woman and does still think of herself that way, we are forced to pretend to the world that she is a man in order to spare us, and all those who work for us, great cruelty at the hands of our cousin."

"Well, at least she knows she's a she, else I'd have had to recommend her to Bedlam," the doctor murmured.

"Is she going to be all right?" Sabrina asked.

The doctor nodded. "Quite a knock to the head, but he'll pull through. No skull damage, luckily. Head wounds just bleed like a sieve."

Sabrina nodded and Anne plopped the carpet bag down on the bed next to the unconscious Sam. "How much to keep this quiet?" she asked.

He frowned at Anne. "Pardon me?"

"How much will it take for you to leave here and tell all the world that you treated a man?" Anne reiterated.

"Madam, I am sure you understand about doctor-patient confidentiality," the doctor said stiffly.

"So, is that a hundred pounds?" Anne haggled, opening the bag.

The doctor put a hand over hers. "Madam, I am paid quite well by this establishment, and Mr. Watts here has already stressed in the strongest possible language how odious Sir Jeremy Acton is. I am not ignorant of a woman's plight in this world, nor of the plight of the poor. I spend many spare hours in the rookeries. I would fain expose this woman, leading to the ruination of not only Miss Acton's, but many other lives. I am a man of science, but I do believe there is a God who watches over all that we do, and I can only think that exposing Sir Acton here would be a terrible sin. I require no money from you."

Anne just stared, frozen with her hand half in the carpet bag.

Sabrina's eyes welled with tears. "Bless you, doctor."

"Dr. Phillip Rogers. If you have need of a doctor again while you are in London, do please contact me. There are other doctors who would have taken your bribe." The doctor gave his card to Sabrina, who handed it to Anne, which startled the woman from her incredulous state.

"We know. There is a doctor near Acton we still bribe regularly to keep him quiet. The one who treated Sir Acton's burns. Of course he knows she's a woman," Anne said faintly.

"Then he is a man of low morals," Dr. Rogers grumped. He turned and snapped his doctor's bag shut. "I recommend leaving her to rest here. When she wakes up, Mr. Watts shall send for me again and I will return to check and make sure she's still in one piece."

"Thank you, Dr. Rogers," Sabrina said. "Really, I cannot thank you enough."

The doctor waved a hand. "It's what I do. Now, Mr. Watts, I suppose we should sort out those two downstairs."

"Must we?" Rick muttered.

"A doctor does not leave his patients in pain if he can help it. Do let me know if she wakes up before I leave." The doctor headed for the door.

"Is it all right for us to stay here tonight and keep watch, Mr. Watts?" Sabrina asked.

"Yes. And I've no doubt your friends downstairs will as well," Rick said.

"Patients with head injuries sometimes say things that are better left unsaid while they are recuperating. If you intend to keep the two men I saw in the dark, I would suggest limiting their visits," the doctor warned.

Anne nodded. "I'll see to it, doctor."

"Good." The doctor nodded to Rick, and the two men left.

Sabrina knelt down next to the bed. "Oh Sam. How did I know you would get yourself into some sort of trouble?"

"You're the one who recommended she take a night out with these people," Anne reminded her.

"True. All right, I rather expected she'd get into a different sort of trouble, but London has been a curse on us since we got here," Sabrina sighed.

"All the more reason to go back to Acton when he's feeling better. We'll close up the London house again and go home," Anne said.

"Yes, Anne. You're right, of course." Sabrina took her sister's hand and brushed some stray blonde hair off her forehead. The pillow beneath her head was red with blood that was oozing through the bandage.

Anne rolled up her sleeves. "Need to re-bandage that wound. At least the doctor will have gotten the glass out, if there was any."

"I wonder if there are clean sheets." Sabrina and Anne began rummaging through cupboards.

There was a knock at the door. "Miss Sabrina? May we come in?" Theo asked on the other side.

Sabrina and Anne looked at each other, then at Sam. "She seems to be in a deep sleep," Anne said slowly. "There mightn't be a better time."

"I agree." Sabrina went to the door and opened it. "Duke Tennant, Lord Hamilton, thank you so much for your continued presence. The doctor says Sam will be all right. He just needs to sleep a bit."

"That's a relief." Callum pushed past Sabrina and went to Sam's bedside. "The doctor thought it would be a good idea to bundle him up in clothes again, cravat and all?"

Oh yes. That. Sabrina chewed her lip. "Sam is very self-conscious about his burns. I would not feel comfortable having company here if they were visible, as Sam would never forgive me."

"I'd think, after taking a knock like that, we'd be more concerned about his physical comfort, but if you're convinced this is what he would want..." Callum said with a frown.

"We are certain, Your Grace," Anne replied firmly.

Theo looked at Sabrina. "Are you all right? There is a bit of blood..."

"I saw what happened to my brother after the fire. There is little that can turn my stomach now," she assured him. "But thank you for your kind concern."

"At least you dispensed with his jacket. These clothes will all need a good wash. I don't suppose you brought a second set?" Callum asked.

"No," Sabrina said without thinking. Then she paled.

"You said there were clothes in that bag," Theo accused. "Why did you lie to me?"

"Because it's none of your business, my Lord," Anne responded testily. "If you must know, it's money. Some doctors don't have many scruples and will tell tales about what they see."

Sabrina held up her hand. "And I'm not commenting on twigs and berries. Suffice to say, the injuries were grievous, and Sam would not want his state spread among society."

"Did you pay him?" Callum asked. "Because you shouldn't have. I would have covered the cost. It is my fault, after all. I started the brawl."

"I thought they did?" Sabrina's eyebrows drew together in confusion.

"They did," Theo insisted. "They were the ones talking about twigs and berries."

"But I threw the first punch," Callum admitted.

"Men," Anne grunted, finding the cabinet she was looking for and beginning to tear a sheet up for bandages. "I hope they're not overly fond of these sheets. As I hope Sir Acton is not overly fond of his attire. Bloodstains are not the easiest to get out of fabric."

"I'll pay for a new set of clothes," Callum said.

Theo protested. "The drunkard should pay for a new set of clothes!"

"We're going home," Sabrina reminded them. "Sam doesn't need any more fine clothes than he already has. This set can simply be deemed a casualty of war."

"Too right it was!" Theo said. "We'd all had quite enough of Jeremy Acton's rumors."

"Careful, Your Grace. You'll get blood on your own clothes." Anne approached the bed and Callum began to unwind Sam's bandage.

"You think I care about clothes? Doubtless Miss Sabrina will ruin her gown before the night is through," he replied.

"Not if I have anything to do with it," Anne said. She grudgingly accepted Callum's help, however, allowing him to hold Sam's head up while she changed bandages.

Sabrina watched Callum with her sister and a strange thought crossed her mind, but she dismissed it. What she was thinking wasn't possible. "You two don't have to stay. Anne and I will watch over Sam."

"We're staying," Callum responded flatly. "And there is nothing you can do about it."

"Tennant! Be polite, at least," Theo scolded him.

"I'm stating facts," Callum said unrepentantly.

"But... I'm not sure Sam would want you to stay," Sabrina gaped, realizing her mistake too late. She hadn't thought that, once they were in, they would refuse to leave.

"You could state them more politely," Theo told him. To Sabrina, he said, "Don't fret. We will all get through this together."

Anne and Sabrina shared a look of concern. "I'm sure you gentlemen have other things to do," Anne tried.

"Not a thing. Nothing as important as making sure Acton stays with us," Callum intoned.

Anne shrugged helplessly at her mistress.

Sabrina sighed. It wasn't as though they could bodily remove them. "The doctor said he might start saying strange things before he's fully recovered. I just want to make sure you're ready for the nonsense."

"Or the truth," Callum said.

She stomped her foot on the floor. "I believe Sam told you he will reveal whatever you wish to hear once I am properly married."

"What if it affects my decision?" he asked.

"Whatever it is will never affect my decision. I've made it, and that is that," Theo stated.

"If it will affect your decision, then there is no competition," Sabrina said primly.

Callum smiled slightly. "There never was, as far as you two are concerned. But I'm staying in this race. Whatever it is you are hiding."

"Then why are you being so stubborn?" Sabrina asked in exasperation.

"Because Acton is my friend."

Since Callum now occupied her brother's bedside, and the other side of the bed was too close to the wall for her to squeeze herself beside Sam, she sat in a chair instead, a hand to her now throbbing forehead. "You make little sense, Your Grace."

"I know." He was still absolutely unrepentant.

Theo went to stand beside Sabrina while Anne poured water from a jug on the vanity into a bowl and began washing away some of the blood on Sam's neck and in his hair outside the bandage.

"The curl in his hair is more pronounced. I suppose that is because his is shorter," Callum observed softly.

Again, suspicion fluttered across Sabrina's consciousness, especially when Theo gave Callum a sharp look.

Anne also frowned, but glanced her way and didn't comment.

"I feel I am not the only one keeping secrets," Sabrina finally said, tired of the strangeness in the air.

"And you are not the only one who will learn about them *after* you are married," Callum replied.

Sabrina scowled, but there was little she could say to that.

Strange Thoughts

Callum

As Sabrina sat in a chair, her eyes drooping as the hours passed, Callum continued to stay by Sam's bedside.

Theo paced and Anne was keeping a weather eye on Sam's bandages, but the bleeding had finally stopped and now things were just crusting.

"Are you sure you're comfortable there?" Sabrina asked tiredly.

Callum realized he'd been kneeling for some time. "I suppose we could get another couple of chairs in here."

"I'll get them," Theo said. He stepped out of the room.

Then it was just Sabrina, Callum, and Anne.

"You are oddly fixated on my brother, I must say," Sabrina finally blurted.

Anne looked at her sharply but Callum shrugged. "Think what you will."

That didn't satisfy her and she asked, "What exactly are your feelings toward my brother?"

"Complicated," was all Callum would answer, despite some follow up questions that he didn't really listen to. Instead, he watched the slow rise and fall of Sam's chest, brooding over his own thoughts.

Those thoughts were going nowhere good. He wanted to know how Sam's skin felt, and how his intact skin would differ from his burned skin. He remembered the touch of Sam's lips, before his friend had, rightly, punched him, and longed to taste them again.

He was certain, if Sam had gone to Eton with Theo and him, Callum would know what it was like to be intimate with another man. It was vexing that these strange feelings were happening now, rather than at a time when everyone was experimenting. He was supposed to be over such things by now, but it seemed it was just beginning.

Callum wanted to reach out and stroke Sam's soft, blond, wavy hair, but he was fairly certain that would just garner more attention from Sabrina than he wanted right now. She was already suspicious, and him hovering over Sam's bedside like an anxious husband wasn't helping. But he couldn't imagine himself anywhere else.

Theo returned with Rick and Dennis and three more chairs. Callum moved just long enough for them to set one at Sam's bedside, and then he was back again.

Anne murmured her thanks as one was placed next to the cabinet for her, and Theo situated his as close to Sabrina as he could without raising eyebrows.

He knew he should object, or be jealous, or something, but Callum just wasn't able to focus on anything but Sam.

Callum also knew he should allow Sabrina to take the bedside place, as would be proper, but he didn't care much about that, either. Strange that he should get attached to the fiery young man so quickly.

It was the wee hours of the morning when Sam started to mumble. "No... mother..."

Callum sat up.

"Hot..." Sam started clawing at his clothes and thrashing a bit. "Hot..."

"We should get him out of his shirt and cravat, at least," Callum said to Sabrina, who had perked up a bit.

"Not the shirt," she replied. "But I don't see any reason to keep the cravat."

"He's hot," Callum argued.

She sighed. "He's dreaming about the fire."

Callum's eyes widened. "All the more reason to take off his clothes."

"Like I said, he'd never forgive me if we did. Cravat only," she insisted.

Anne and Theo were also giving him hard looks, so, with a sigh of his own, Callum gently removed Sam's cravat, revealing more scarring, of course.

Sam continued to thrash until Callum put a hand on his arm. "Everything is fine," he said calmly. "You're safe. There is no fire."

At the sound of his voice, Sam quieted and slipped back into sleep.

Sabrina blinked at him, but Callum didn't comment. He was just glad it had worked.

Two hours later, Sam finally opened his brilliant blue eyes. Theo had fallen asleep in his chair, and Anne and Sabrina were struggling to stay awake. But Callum was focused, and when Sam's eyes opened, he leaned forward quickly. "Acton!" He turned to the others. "He's awake!"

Sabrina and Anne stood and crowded around him, while Theo struggled to wake up. "Sam!" Sabrina said, grabbing his hand. "Are you all right?!"

"Not so loud," Sam croaked.

This time, Sabrina did lower her voice. "The doctor said you were going to be okay, and to call him when you woke up so he could assess you again."

Sam paled. "Doctor?"

"A good doctor, your lordship," Anne said quickly. "It's all sorted. No need to worry."

Sam relaxed with a groan.

"Why are you so worried about the doctor?" Callum asked.

But Sam was sharp enough now to deflect the question. "Scars," he said simply.

"See? Now you can stop being so suspicious," Anne harrumphed.

"Right." Callum was still unconvinced, but he was completely stymied now.

"I'll go send for the doctor," Theo said, rising.

"Thank you," Sabrina said.

Callum squeezed Sam's shoulder. "You took quite a knock to the head."

"I kind of thought so," Sam grunted, then winced. "Talking... is not good."

Callum nodded and fell silent.

Overheard Conversations

Sabrina

Sabrina paused outside the parlor door, shocked stiff. Though she was not entirely sure what "bugger" meant, from the context, she deduced it had something to do with having relations with a man.

She almost didn't catch the rest of it, she was so busy processing that one word. But when she finally did manage to draw breath again, she realized that Callum was, indeed, in love with her sister.

That was problematic for a myriad of reasons.

Careful not to rustle her skirts, she backed away from the parlor door, bumping right into Anne who had come to chaperone. Anne was also looking scandalized, but not confused. Not confused at all.

Sabrina put a finger to her lips and took Anne by the wrist back up the stairs to her bedroom. "What's going on, Anne?" she asked. "What are they talking about? Greece and Rome and b-bug—"

"Don't say it, your ladyship. "'Tis a very filthy word," Anne said quickly.

"What does it mean, then?" Sabrina put her hands on her hips and frowned so Anne knew she would take no nonsense.

Anne pressed her lips together. "It's not my place to be telling you the ways of men and women, and certainly not men and men."

"That man is courting me while talking about an obsession of some kind he has with Sam. I demand to know what's going on," she said. "And I know about the 'ways of men and women.' Sam wanted to make sure I wasn't naive or frightened on my wedding night and took pains to acquire an anatomy book when we were sixteen."

The maid grimaced. "If your ladyship knows about men's anatomy, it should be no great leap to think how a man might lay with another man."

It took several seconds of silence, but Sabrina's nose finally wrinkled and she had to sit down. "That's rather unsavory."

"There's types in this world who love their own kind. It happens a lot more than you would think," Anne sighed. "I'm not one to condone such things, but they do happen."

"And Callum wants to do this... thing... with my sister," Sabrina said faintly.

"With your brother. And I have a notion if he knew your brother was actually your sister, he'd be quite relieved," Anne explained. "In fact, maybe somewhere at the back of his mind he already knows. It sounds to me from their conversation that he's not ever wanted a man before."

Sabrina's expression turned thoughtful. "I'd like for Sam to be happy, and if His Grace doesn't mind her burns..."

Anne sat down next to Sabrina on her bed and took her hands. "You can't be forgetting about Sir Jeremy Acton."

Her musings disappeared in a puff of horror. "No. You're right. Sam is all that stands between several innocent lives and misery. Not to mention, Jeremy would likely consider it his right to approve or not approve my marriage. And hers."

"'Tis a saintly thing your sister has undertaken," Anne said quietly. "And a lonely trap it is." She bit her lip. "Perhaps after you're properly wedded, Miss Samantha could find her way to marrying His Grace before Sir Acton found out."

"That would still leave Acton at Jeremy's mercy. Sam would never allow it." Sabrina looked sad. "I thought Sam needed to be a man because there was no other choice for her. It breaks my heart that we were wrong all this time."

"Miss Samantha deserves all the happiness this world has to offer," Anne replied. "Your father just didn't think it would be possible for a man to look at her the way His Grace does. But, on the other hand, your ladyship, if Miss Samantha had been raised any differently, she would not have caught His Grace's attention."

Sabrina held her head in her hands and groaned. "What do we do now that she has?"

"I think that we're in the same situation as His Grace. We don't know, and we don't know how Miss Samantha feels about it, regardless," Anne said. "And don't you go messing your hair. It will take forever to put it up again!"

"I'll need to speak with her at the earliest possible opportunity." Sabrina carefully extricated her fingers from her hair. "I wish I could talk to her right this moment!"

"You can't. You've two gentlemen to entertain." Anne rose and held out her hand to Sabrina, helping her to her feet.

"How am I supposed to pretend I didn't hear that sordid conversation?" Sabrina asked.

Anne took her by the shoulders. "Your sister pretends every day that she is a man. You can smile and be charming for the span of one breakfast."

Sabrina decided Anne was right. She squared her shoulders and marched out her bedroom door in front of her maid.

Theo and Callum stood when Sabrina entered the parlor, Anne just behind her.

"Thank you for waiting, gentlemen," Sabrina said with a demure smile. "Please, let us go to the dining room for breakfast."

The men nodded and followed as she turned around and started toward the dining room, Anne now ahead of her.

There was toast, coffee, several kinds of preserves, and tea set out on the table. Theo rushed to pull out Sabrina's chair for her, for which she was relieved, because she had no idea what expression would have crossed her face if Callum had tried to do it.

For his part, Callum was brooding, not quite paying attention when Sabrina and Theo began to engage in lighthearted conversation about fishing.

From time to time, Sabrina flicked her gaze Callum's way, trying to divine what he was thinking. She liked that Theo was more of an open book.

Anne hovered, serving the three of them while she acted as chaperone. She, too, glanced from time to time at Callum, who hadn't even yet acknowledged there was toast and tea in front of him.

"I should really go back to see your brother," Callum finally said, his expression still troubled.

Sabrina stood. "Actually, I was thinking the same, and would beg an hour alone with him, if you don't mind."

Callum raised an eyebrow and really looked at Sabrina for the first time that morning. "Why?"

"Tennant, it's her brother. If she wants an hour with him, you give her an hour with him," Theo put in, giving Callum a significant look. "And don't let him put you off your breakfast, Miss Sabrina. We'll all finish and go to the club together. You can go upstairs to your brother, and we will wait below. This one owes me a rematch at backgammon, anyway."

She was so grateful she could have kissed him, but then Anne would have been scandalized and Callum... well, it was difficult to say what Callum would have thought. "Thank you, Lord Hamilton." She sat back down, but did hurry in eating her toast and drinking her coffee, lest Callum decide to go against Theo's admonition and go see Sam before she got a chance to.

When everyone was finished, Anne quickly swept the table clean and got Sabrina ready to travel. "You two gentlemen ought to go home and scrub up a bit. It's not my place to say, but you look like hell," she said to Callum and Theo. "That should give Miss Sabrina enough time with Sir Acton."

"Good idea," Theo agreed. "Come along, Tennant. We probably smell like a sewer and look even worse."

Callum grumbled under his breath, but reluctantly followed his friend out to hail a carriage.

Anne and Sabrina took a second carriage back to the club. Rick was still there looking after Sam. He quietly left the room when Anne and Sabrina entered.

"Thank you!" Sabrina called after him.

Sam was asleep, but this matter took precedence, so Sabrina went to her bedside and gave her shoulder a shake.

Sam moaned and blinked bloodshot eyes open. "Where's the fire?" she mumbled.

"Listen," Sabrina said. "I don't have a lot of time to tell you this and discuss it, so I'll just have to go ahead. His Grace is in love with you."

"Tennant?" Sam asked sleepily, blinking herself awake. "Where did you get an idea like that?"

"I overheard him talking to Lord Hamilton. But that's not the point. He's intent on... having you," she continued, uncomfortable.

Sam snorted. "I highly doubt that. He thinks I'm a man."

"He was talking about b-b—!" Sabrina tried to get the word out.

"Buggery," Anne provided helpfully.

That got Sam's full attention. "What?!"

"Yes, that," Sabrina said. "He's very confused. He likes you more than one man should like another, but it sounds as though that's never happened to him before, so either he loves you that much as a person or..."

"... or on some level he knows you're a woman," Anne finished.

Sam sat straight up. "No. No, no, no!"

"He's been very attentive this entire time you've been asleep. It's rather endearing, in a way, but also... Sam, I don't know what we're going to do," Sabrina said.

"Well, obviously, Miss Sabrina will have to marry Lord Hamilton," Anne assumed.

"Obviously not," Sam replied.

"What?!" the other two women squawked.

Sam shook her head, then winced, regretting it. "If Sabrina marries Hamilton, I've sworn to reveal my secret to Tennant. He might take that mistakenly as my being... available? I don't know, this has all become hopelessly complicated now."

"What would be so wrong about that?" Sabrina demanded.

"Sir Jeremy. The estate," Anne reminded her.

"Yes, precisely," Sam said.

Sabrina huffed. "You want to trap Duke Tennant into a marriage with me, then? So that he can't marry you?"

"He can't marry me anyway." Sam threw off the covers and turned, wincing again. "But it would be one possible solution."

"I won't marry him, Sam. Especially now," Sabrina said.

"Ugh. Not so loud." Sam put a hand to her head. "We need to go home. Now."

"You're also telling Lord Hamilton. And don't try to argue the point. It is my price for marrying *anybody*." Sabrina folded her arms over her chest.

Sam glared at her. "And you think he'll keep the secret?"

"Not from Duke Tennant, but from everyone else? Yes," Sabrina insisted. "And lay down, you fool, we're not going anywhere for two days. You invited them to the estate, remember? It will look quite suspicious if we go running there like scared rabbits."

"Do lay down, your ladyship," Anne said, already manhandling Sam onto her back. "It's not all so terrible that we need to go risking your health."

Sam groaned and closed her eyes. "What a mess."

"Yes," Sabrina agreed. "What a mess, indeed."

To Acton

Theo

It was an awkward two days.

When Theo and Callum arrived after breakfasting at Eleven Charles Place, Sam had been awake, but... odd. He looked bothered by something, but when Callum or Theo asked, he insisted it was nothing.

If Callum hadn't turned to politics, Theo wasn't sure the suddenly recalcitrant man would have spoken at all.

Sabrina was also not herself. Her smile had become strained and she was also more quiet than usual. If it weren't for her continued passionate, furtive glances at him, Theo would have thought she'd stopped caring.

The ride to Acton was strange to say the least. Sam winced at every little rock and bump of the carriage, while Sabrina watched her brother carefully and squeezed his hand while he was in pain.

Callum had, wisely, decided not to talk politics in the carriage. In fact, due to Sam's condition, there was a rather stern ban on any talking at all.

"Maybe we should have stayed in London a few more days," Theo whispered to Sabrina.

"No," Sam said, his voice tight. "Not one more minute."

Sabrina shrugged at Theo, though when Sam closed his eyes, she mouthed 'we should have stayed.'

The hours crawled by until, mercifully, they stopped at an inn for the night. Though that started a whole new set of problems.

"Acton shouldn't stay alone with no one watching him," Callum announced at dinner in the dining room. "I will room with him. Just in case."

Both the Actons paled and looked at each other. "That won't be necessary," Sam said, sipping at his stew. "I will be perfectly fine on my own. You might room with Hamilton, though."

"Anne and I will be close by," Sabrina added. "There's no need to worry."

"There is every need," Callum insisted angrily. "Just what is the matter with you two? You're jumping at every little thing and all I get is the most terse of civility. Hamilton as well."

Sabrina looked at Sam, who pushed his stew aside and folded his hands on the tabletop. "I am not open to the kind of relationship Sabrina heard you describing at our London home the other day."

It was Callum's turn to pale and Theo's jaw dropped. "You heard that?" Theo said, looking at Sabrina.

"Anne had to explain some of it to me, but I understood the gist," Sabrina replied primly, smoothing and rearranging her napkin in her lap. "We were trying to be polite, but I suppose we missed the mark somewhere along the way. It's all out in the open now, though."

"Acton, I... I'm sorry," Callum stuttered. "I... wasn't even quite sure myself... that is to say..."

"I will take it as the affectionate gesture it was meant to be," Sam interrupted him. "But, for a number of reasons, not the least of which being you are courting my sister, I cannot engage in such an affair with you."

"Of course," Callum said gruffly.

"And I hope, regardless, we can still be friends," Sam went on after a pause.

Callum looked up and the hope on his face was almost painful, in Theo's opinion. "You'd really allow that?"

"I did not go to Eton, but I am not ignorant," Sam said. "Let us stay friends. I would dearly miss our conversations."

"Thank you, Acton," Callum replied, a smile of relief on his face.

"So, does that mean I'm ahead in the running now?" Theo tried to joke.

The other three grimaced at him, and he held up his hands. "I'm just kidding."

"Your sense of humor often leaves something to be desired," Sam sighed. "But my sister likes you, anyway. That is no small thing."

"Am I still being considered?" Callum asked cautiously.

"Yes." Sam gave Sabrina a look when it seemed she was about to say 'no.'

Callum chuckled. "That's not happiness on Miss Sabrina's part. I promise, fair maiden, if I cannot win you over while we are at Acton, I will graciously bow out."

"Good," Sabrina said, somewhat mollified.

The sour mood that had descended over Theo brightened, and it seemed a great weight had been lifted off the table as a whole.

❧

THE FOLLOWING DAY SEEMED JUST AS PAINFUL FOR SAM, BUT the others did take to whispered conversations. When Callum would have turned the conversation to the Great Stink and the abysmal state of London's sewer system, Theo and Sabrina steered him quickly away. Sam was too primed to jump into the conversation, and no one wanted his head hurting any more than it already was.

Acton came into view over a hill, sprawling and beautiful. There was nothing particularly grand about the small mansion on the property. But the way the people smiled and waved when the carriage rolled by and the cheerful efficiency with which they were met at the mansion made it seem a very happy place indeed.

Once ensconced back in his home environment, Sam seemed much more at ease, which put Sabrina at ease once more. She was the quintessential hostess, and Theo found himself even more in love with her now that he could see her in the comfort of her own home, than he had been in London. He decided, after properly showing Sabrina the delights of London, he wouldn't mind so much being at home more than he was in the city. Not as long as she was at Kilgore with him.

"Might I trouble you for a walk in the gardens, Miss Sabrina?" Theo asked once everyone was settled and had eaten.

"Is Duke Tennant also coming along?" Sabrina asked hesitantly.

Callum laughed. "Go on, then. I can see when I'm not wanted."

This surprised Theo, but then, Callum had stopped anything that could be considered acts of courtship toward Sabrina ever since the candid conversation at the inn. Theo wondered what his game was.

"I'll just see if Marta's about," Sabrina said, rising.

The other three rose as well. "Anne isn't coming?" Theo asked.

"Anne has much to do now that we're home. Marta is the upstairs maid." Sabrina dropped her voice a bit lower. "She's somewhat lazy, but I think she'd enjoy a turn in the garden as much as anyone else."

"All right. I'll see you soon," Theo smiled.

Sabrina bustled out of the sitting room to go find Marta.

Sam looked up from his book and speared Theo with a look. "I won't have you taking advantage of Marta's distractedness. Do you understand?"

"I wouldn't dream of it," Theo said, injecting as much innocence into his tone as he could.

"Right," Sam muttered, but went back to his reading.

Callum put down one corner of his paper to give Theo the same look. "Don't go taking liberties."

"You two, honestly. What could I possibly do with a distractible chaperone there?" Theo teased.

Neither of the men seemed impressed by his joke.

"I'll be good," Theo promised.

"I'll hold you to that," Sam said.

Sabrina returned with a very dowdy, droopy-eyed maid whom Theo assumed must be Marta. "Sleeping already at this time of day. Honestly."

"I was up late last night making ready, your ladyship," Marta defended herself.

"And whose fault is that? You had three days to make ready," Sabrina admonished her.

Marta pouted, but fell silent.

Theo tried not to grin at Marta's predicament. He held out his arm to Sabrina. "Shall we, Miss Sabrina?"

"I would be delighted, Lord Hamilton," Sabrina said.

Sabrina directed them out to the gardens, Marta trailing behind with a yawn. There were some roses and deliberately cultivated flowering plants here and there, but for the most part, the gardener had left the place to grow bursting with wildflowers with a tame path in between.

"It is a very fine evening," Theo remarked, glancing back at Marta, who was falling more and more behind as she plodded along behind them.

"Yes, very," she agreed. "Not too warm with a nice breeze."

"And now shall we discuss the roads?" he teased.

She laughed. "Perhaps we should discuss the very romantic Great Stink in London. Duke Tennant seemed to think it was proper conversation."

"I do wish he hadn't brought up cholera over dinner, but I suppose if you would like to discuss it in depth..." he grinned.

"No, thank you. Putting me off my dinner was quite enough." Sabrina led him to a small, secluded area of the garden with a tall oak tree and a white, wrought iron bench beneath it.

Theo raised an eyebrow at the bench, then looked behind them again, only to find Marta pulling thistles out of her skirt. How she had managed to tromp through them when they'd been perfectly obvious was beyond him.

"Do sit down," Sabrina said, and they sat together, side-by-side, on the bench. Marta was still plucking thistles from her skirt, so Theo took the opportunity to quickly drop a kiss on her lips.

She gasped. "Lord Hamilton!"

"Are you terribly scandalized?" Theo asked contritely.

Sabrina looked back at Marta, who had managed to tumble into a hedgerow, and placed her hand on Theo's. "Not terribly, no," she replied with a blush.

"I think I like Marta better than Anne," Theo whispered.

"I think I shall be ever grateful hereafter for bumbling chaperones," she agreed.

Marta finally managed to untangle herself and walked over to the couple in a huff. Sabrina surreptitiously removed her hand from Theo's before Marta could see they'd been touching. "What did I miss?" the maid asked.

Theo and Sabrina looked at each other and smiled. "Oh, nothing."

Restless

Sam

Sam finished reading the passage she'd been on in her book and stretched. "I think I'll go for a wall on one of the woodland trails. Would you like to come?"

Callum looked up from his paper. "Hmm. Not just now, I don't think. I think someone should keep an eye on our happy couple."

"Marta is there," Sam pointed out.

Callum snorted. "Marta is not exactly the best of chaperones, I don't think."

"Probably not." She frowned. "Perhaps I should go out to the garden myself."

"No. Go for your walk. I'm sure if there's trouble, it's nothing myself and Anne can't handle," he smiled.

She chewed her lip a moment, then nodded. "I'll be back before sundown. Please, feel free to wander wherever you wish."

"I shall," he said. "Enjoy your walk."

"Thank you." She went to change into a good pair of walking boots, then headed out for the woods.

Sam was actually happy Callum had decided not to come. She

needed time and space to think. It had become a much tougher question than it had been before - who to marry Sabrina to. On the one hand, Sabrina was very taken with Theo, but Theo didn't strike Sam as much of a secret-keeper despite what Sabrina thought. And Theo was less titled, less connected, and had less money than Callum.

Callum was being brought into the fold regardless. Sam had already promised him that. However, what would happen now that he had deeper feelings for Sam the man, and he found out she was actually Samantha the woman? There were a thousand things that could go wrong if they didn't lock him into the conspiracy through marriage.

With her mind occupied by such thoughts, Sam tripped on a tree root and went skidding down the side of a ravine, through mud and debris, tearing her shirt, pants, and vest in places.

Swearing, Sam stood at the bottom of the ravine and surveyed the damage. She herself wasn't too scratched up, but her clothes were in ruins.

She was also muddy from head to toe, with little leaves and pine needles sticking to her.

Luckily, there was a stream at the bottom of the ravine. Sam stomped over to it and peeled off her vest and shirt, leaving her in only the bindings that flattened her breasts. She washed mud and a little blood off her arms and face, then began scrubbing mud out of torn shirt and vest.

The crack of a twig alerted Sam to the presence of something or someone else, and she slowly turned her head.

To her horror, Sabrina and Theo were standing at the top of the ravine!

Sam snatched her wet shirt back on, but it simply stuck to her bindings, visible through the shirt. As were her scars.

"Um..." Theo was gaping, one hand on a tree branch. He'd clearly been about to descend to help her.

"Shit," Sam swore.

Sabrina's hands were covering her mouth, her eyes wide with disbelief.

"I think... maybe... you should come up here," Theo said as reasonably as any of them could manage in that awkward moment. "And... we should discuss a few things."

"And take that wet thing off you before you catch a cold along with a concussion," Sabrina added, rallying.

Sam grimaced and peeled the shirt back off. It had now also soaked her bindings but, thankfully, those were thick enough and made of a sturdy enough material that nothing underneath could be seen even when they were wet. "I'm going to need another shirt and vest," she said to Marta, who finally came around the path. "Go back and get them, please."

Marta gawped at Sam for a good minute before the words registered, then she turned and scurried faster than she might ever have moved in her life.

Digging her boots into the muck, Sam climbed back up the ravine, grabbing branches and skinny trees as she passed them to aid in her ascent.

Theo moved a third of the way down the ravine to offer her a hand, but Sam declined it. "Thank you, I'm fine," she said.

"You're not a man, are you," Theo wheezed once they were back on the path.

"Well-spotted," she replied tersely.

"Sam, at least be polite," Sabrina admonished her.

"You said you were going for a walk in the gardens," Sam accused.

"The gardens are only just so big! I thought we could continue our walk in the woods," Sabrina replied defensively.

Theo cleared his throat. "Can we get back to the part where you're not actually a man? That's really my sticking point right now, not where we all decided to be walking today."

"What is there to tell? I am Sabrina's twin sister. There you have it," Sam said, crossing her arms over her flattened chest.

"Why?" Theo asked.

"Well, you see, when a man and a woman love each other very much..." Sam began sarcastically.

Sabrina rolled her eyes. "Sam. Be nice. And explain, or I will."

Her jaw worked. "My father didn't have any sons, and he was unwilling to marry again after our stepmother died. Luckily, the fire made me unmarriageable, so it was a simple thing to change me from a girl to a boy."

"But... why?" Theo asked again.

"Jeremy Acton," the women said together.

Theo blinked, then after a few moments, realization dawned. "He would have inherited the estate upon your father's death."

"And been responsible for our wellbeing. And marriages," Sabrina said. "That would have been awful."

"How... how do people not know? Wasn't there some sort of birth announcement?" Theo asked.

"Our mother died in childbirth. My father thought it was too solemn an event to be overshadowed by a joyful birth announcement. He met our stepmother when he still traveled for business, and she died in the fire that nearly killed me when I was five," Sam explained. "After that, there was nothing that could induce my father to leave the estate, and it became a great secret among those who work on the estate. No one wanted Jeremy to inherit and take over the estate, cruel, stupid man that he is. So everyone went along with it. We do still have to bribe the local doctor from time to time, but..."

"It would be clever if it weren't so awful," Theo said quietly.

Sam looked at Sabrina, then back at Theo. "What do you mean, awful?"

"Well, for you to have to pretend to be something that you're not," Theo responded.

That made her laugh. "Hamilton, I've been a boy since I was five years old. There is very little I have to put effort into anymore to 'make-believe' I am a man. Though these bindings are quite awful, I would agree."

"I imagine they are painful." Theo sat himself down on a stump, still looking gobsmacked. "The doctor at the club, he knew. Anne brought that money to bribe him. And Rick, because he's marrying, who... Jenny... from your estate, he knew and helped to cover it up."

"Yes, quite a lot more people than I'd like know, but there is nothing I can do about that," Sam said. "The question now, of course, is what do you intend to do with the information?"

"Pardon?" Theo replied.

"Are you going to tell Duke Tennant?" Sabrina clarified for her sister.

Theo frowned. "Why wouldn't I?"

"See, I told you," Sam said, triumphant and bitter in the same breath.

Sabrina put her hands on her hips. "Theodore Hamilton, you will do *no* such thing. Sam has promised to tell Duke Tennant her secret *after* I am properly married."

"Tennant is my best friend," Theo argued.

"I'm your future wife," she replied.

"I don't know that Sam has decided that. If it's even his—her—decision to make." Theo eyed Sam critically, like she was some strange, exotic species of bird in a zoo.

Sabrina's hands flew to her mouth once more. "What are you saying? Are you going to tell Jeremy?"

Theo examined Sam a while longer, then looked up at Sabrina. "No," he finally said at length. "You're right. That man is a monster and doesn't deserve to have charge of an estate like Acton."

"Are you going to hold my feet to the fire now and demand I let you marry Sabrina?" Sam rejoined.

"I should," Theo said after a pause. "That would be the cunning move, I suppose. But no, I'm not going to do that, either. But I am going to tell you that you need to tell Tennant the truth *before* any wedding takes place, no matter who the groom is going to be."

"That's... a bit... problematic..." Sam started.

"It's the price of my silence." Theo's eyes narrowed on Sam. "You are doing Tennant a great disservice by pretending. He thinks he's in love with a man."

Sam raised her chin. "For all practical intents and purposes, he is. Though I doubt he feels quite *that* strongly."

"Then you have not been paying attention." Theo glanced at Sabrina. "Would it not be better to see if I might marry Miss Sabrina while Tennant marries..."

"I'd just continue to call myself Acton. It makes things less confusing. And you are forgetting Jeremy," Sam reminded him.

"Jeremy." Theo's brow furrowed in thought. "Yes, he would take custody of this land."

"He would drag Sam through the mud *and* make her pay in some way for robbing him these many years of his inheritance," Sabrina pointed out. "If she didn't end up in prison, she'd end up in Bedlam."

Theo looked even more puzzled. "I see where this has become such a predicament."

"Tennant is never going to marry a woman who looks like this." Sam gestured to her scarring. "And if I don't play Samuel Acton until the day I die, everyone's happiness is put at risk."

"Yet you give no thought to your own happiness," Theo said softly. "And I feel it is a bit insulting to assume Tennant could not look past your scars."

"We're never going to find out." Sam marched up and grabbed him by the cravat. "Never. Do you hear me?"

"You said you were going to tell Tennant before the wedding," Theo reminded her.

"After. I said after. You said before."

Sabrina pried her away from Theo. "Sam, you're making it sound as though you're having second thoughts about telling him at all."

She pressed her lips into a thin line.

"Sam, you promised!" Sabrina exclaimed.

"That was before this whole love business got thrown into the pot!" Sam shouted back.

Suddenly, Theo laughed, breaking up the fight.

"What's so damned funny?" Sam asked.

"Just... it's so obvious now that you are sisters," he chuckled.

"Yes, well, we always have been. We shared a womb, for heaven's sake," Sam grumbled.

Marta then returned with a shirt, cravat, and vest for her. "Sorry, your lordship. I ran as fast as I could."

"It's fine, Marta. We had much to discuss, anyway," Sam said. She pulled on the clothes.

"You do know your pants are still ripped." Sabrina pointed.

"Yes, I did feel a bit of a breeze." Sam sighed and shook her head. "The top was the most important part, I thought."

"Tennant's going to wonder what happened to you," Theo said.

"Then I'll tell him I fell down the ravine," she replied.

"You should tell him you're a woman is what you should do. He's smart. He'll know what to do about it," Theo suggested.

"Woman? No, your lordship. No woman here but Miss Sabrina," Marta said quickly.

They all just looked at her.

"I thought she was just slow-bodied," Theo whispered to Sabrina.

She swatted him.

"Back to the house, then," Sam said. She began trudging back down the path.

Sabrina and Theo followed, with a very confused Marta bringing up the rear.

"I just don't like keeping secrets from Tennant," Theo murmured to Sabrina as they walked.

"I'll marry him to spite you if you don't, I swear I will," Sabrina hissed back.

Theo smiled slightly. "No, you wouldn't."

Sabrina rolled her eyes, but smiled back. "No, I wouldn't."

"Are you two *quite* finished?" Sam groaned. "You're giving me a headache."

Theo and Sabrina just laughed.

Keeping Secrets

Theo

Not telling Callum about Sam—Samantha—was the hardest thing Theo had ever done in his life.

It was made harder by the fact that Callum was still infatuated with Sam, evidenced by their return from the woods. He saw a scratch on Sam's cheek and immediately went to touch him. He'd been so terribly concerned.

Theo wanted nothing more than to tell his conflicted friend that everything was all right, this had nothing to do with Ancient Greece and Rome. He had genuinely, in fact, fallen in love with a woman.

The threat of losing Sabrina was the only thing that kept him holding his tongue.

Days passed in a lazy sort of way at Acton. With nothing of the hustle and bustle of London around them, Theo went on long walks with Sabrina and, occasionally, riding as well. She pointed out all her favorite places and he met a good number of workers. And Sabrina knew all their names.

He decided that was something he was remiss about on his own estate, and would have to change it. The people worked for him, after all. He should at least know their names. Theo also thought of how lovely it would be to ride in his barouche with Sabrina about his lands, meeting everyone and learning their names.

Callum seemed to have given up on courting Sabrina, but spent many days exploring the property, and, especially, the mansion. When Sam went for his—her—walks, he often stayed behind and poked around. That was likely because Sam took five or six walks a day. How many could one be expected to join her on?

"It's to clear his head," Sabrina said softly when Callum and Theo looked at each other on the third day in surprise while Sam went outside yet again.

"He must have a lot of thoughts," Theo replied. "He's out there most of the time."

"I know for a fact he has a lot of thoughts," Callum added. "Though I've never seen someone so determined to run from them."

"Run from them?!" Sabrina and Theo echoed together, both worried Callum might be discovering more than he should.

Callum shrugged. "Your brother is quite troubled. I'm surprised you've never noticed before."

"Oh." Sabrina glanced at Theo.

Theo could imagine a good number of things that troubled Sam, none of which he could voice to Callum without going down a forbidden path.

"Your brother really isn't going to take a wife?" Callum asked.

That made Theo choke on his tea.

Sabrina gave him a warning glare. "He really isn't. I just don't think he has feelings like that, you know?"

Callum raised an eyebrow. "You don't think your brother is capable of romantic feelings?"

"I... well... no," Sabrina said after giving it some thought.

"You really do think less of him than you do of yourself."

"What?!" Sabrina squawked.

He folded up his paper and stood, tucking it under his arm. "You two enjoy your time. I'm going to go explore the house a bit more. It seems Marta has fallen asleep, so you shouldn't have any trouble stealing kisses this time."

"Callum Tennant, you get back here and explain yourself!" Sabrina demanded, but he didn't turn around and just continued out the sitting room door and up the stairs.

Theo moved to sit over on the settee with her, glancing at the snoring Marta before taking her hands in his. "He's just grumpy because Sam rejected him, Sabrina, that's all."

Sabrina's eyes swam with tears. "I don't think so, Theo. I think he thinks I'm quite selfish. That I don't care if Sam is happy."

"Sam herself—"

"Himself. Callum is still in the house, after all," she whispered quickly.

"Sam *himself* laid out all the reasons why it would be impossible. And he's never expressed any interest in Tennant... that way. I really do think it's because Tennant is bitter," he reassured her.

Her eyebrows drew together and, glancing at the still-sleeping Marta, laid her head on Theo's shoulder. "But... what if *you're* right?"

"Hmm?" he said.

"What if Sam *could* marry Duke Tennant?" Sabrina asked slowly. "And I could marry you and we'd... I don't know... we'd figure *something* out about Acton."

"Jeremy," Theo reminded her. "Do you see him graciously allowing the two of you to be happy after denying him his inheritance all these years? Or magically growing a kinder attitude toward those in his charge?"

She sighed heavily. "No."

"Then your brother has quite a bit of wisdom. Some things are sad, Sabrina, but entirely beyond our control," he replied heavily.

"We must have him at Kilgore as often as possible. Especially once we have our first son. I fear he will not soldier through otherwise," she said with a swallow.

"Tennant mentioned something that led me to believe Sam might do himself a harm," he murmured. "I am sorry for that, Sabrina. I am sorry for his pain."

"I want Sam to be happy. I cannot imagine being a man all these years when you know you are a woman. I mean, there are all the advantages, surely, but... I would not feel right within myself. It would give rise to a very restless spirit in me," she confessed.

Theo glanced back the way Callum had gone. "Hence, as Tennant said, your brother is troubled."

"Sam deserves all the best things in this life, love surely being chief among them. To close off one's heart so harshly, without hope of ever finding... I just..." Tears rolled down Sabrina's cheeks. "I wish for her to just once feel the way I feel when I'm with you."

"Him," he quietly corrected her.

"You know, Anne is supposed to be running a household," came the annoyed voice of Sam. "But if I can't trust you two together, and Marta is going to go nodding off all the time, I'm going to have to pull her away from her duties to keep an eye on the two of you."

The two lovers sprang apart, Theo going straight back to the chair he'd been sitting in, Sabrina sitting up straighter on the settee.

Sam pointedly settled herself down on the settee, glowering at Theo. "And, from what I could hear from the doorway, it seems I am the most interesting topic of conversation today?"

"We were just talking about your happiness," Sabrina said, dabbing her eyes with a handkerchief with Theo's monogram on it.

"Will you please leave my happiness to me." Sam sighed and picked up her book off the table, a French work by the political writer Jean-Jacques Rousseau. "I assure you, I am fine."

"But you're not, Sam." Sabrina clutched her sister's arm. "You're living some twisted little half-life and it's just awful. Don't you hate it, Sam? I hate it for you."

With an angry sound, Sam pulled her arm free. "Can't a man read his book in peace?"

"Sam," Theo said. "Sabrina and I are just concerned—"

"Ugh. Yes, fine already. I have been well aware for the past few days that there is no prying you from the family tree. You have my blessing. Start planning a wedding, if you must, but please, leave me be!" Sam stood, tucking her book under her arm much like Callum had with his paper. "I'm going to find someplace quiet to read. If you need me, I'll be in the study."

"Sam." Sabrina tried to grab for her sister's wrist, but she snatched it away.

"See to your own happiness," she barked, then stalked out of the room.

Theo looked at Sabrina, at the sleeping Marta, at the retreating Sam, then went and perched himself on the settee again.

Sabrina took his hands immediately, squeezing them, the handkerchief with his monogram trapped in between.

"At least she's given us her blessing?" He tried to sound cheerful, but it fell a bit flat.

"Why is it I don't feel happy, then?" she sniffled. A tear rolled down her cheek.

"Oh, my poor love. We'll figure something out. Especially once Callum knows. He'll know what to do," he whispered, touching his forehead to hers.

"Oi! Aren't you two a bit close?" Marta asked, coming awake with a loud snort.

"It's all right, Marta. We're engaged now. Sam gave her blessing," Sabrina said.

Marta's eyes bulged and she looked around. "Oh. His Grace isn't here."

"No. He left a while ago," Theo told her.

"Oh." Marta glanced around some more. "His lordship's book is gone. Did you put it away?"

"Sam's been here and gone, too, Marta," Sabrina responded kindly.

"Oh." She blinked at the couple, who hadn't moved one bit. "So... you say you're engaged now?"

"Yes, quite," Theo said.

"Right then. That's good." Marta settled back in her chair, closed her eyes, and was soon snoring again.

158

"Right then. That's good." Marta settled back in her chair, closed her eyes, and was soon snoring again.

A Picture's Worth

Callum

Meandering the halls of Acton Manor was all that was keeping Callum from going crazy. It was hard being around Sam, enjoying their debates, then remembering he couldn't have him.

In the hopes of Sam's attitude changing about that, he'd stopped courting Sabrina altogether. She and Theo were completely infatuated with each other anyway.

He wasn't sure if Sam had noticed, however. The man went on more walks than were healthy for the constitution, surely. Callum wondered why Sam was more restless here than in London, even though he'd been pining to be back at Acton the entire time he'd been in the city.

Perhaps Callum was the answer? He wondered if he made Sam as restless as Sam made him.

It was the sixth day at Acton when Callum ran out of rooms he was allowed to explore, leaving Sabrina's, Sam's, Theo's, and the servants' quarters untouched as they were private. Desperate for something to do that didn't involve watching Theo and Sabrina make eyes at each other in the sitting room, Callum finally found his way to the attic. Anne had been reluctant to show him there, but the girl Marta had been most helpful.

What could be wrong with exploring a dusty old attic? If he returned full of dust, moths, and spiders' webs, well, that would be his own fault. Callum found himself curious about family portraits that may have been removed, styled clothing from long-gone eras, perhaps even cousin Percy's favorite spoon. Such oddities were sure to hold his interest for at least a couple of afternoons.

The attic was indeed packed with odds and ends for him to explore. There was a particularly sour-looking portrait of a dowdy spinster aunt that made him laugh. One trousseau held the portrait of the daughter of a long-dead baronet of Acton who was lovely, but had been taken down from the hallowed halls because of her elopement with a blacksmith. Callum imagined it had been quite the scandal in its day.

Moth-eaten powdered wigs were strewn over one antique cabinet, while all forms of formalwear hung in different, out-of-fashion armoires.

He was enjoying looking over the different men's and women's shoes from days long past, when he spotted a rather more modern trunk tucked away behind a dress form and some curtains. Curious, he dug the trunk out and dragged it to the middle of the dusty floor, creating a long track behind his footprints.

Callum started to pull at the top of it, however, the trunk was locked.

This only made him smile, however. At last, a puzzle! Perhaps it would take him hours. Perhaps it would take him days. But he would open this trunk.

He began searching the area the trunk had come from for a key, shaking the curtains to no avail. He then began patting down the various clothing and shoes, starting at the most modern and working his way back through time.

Then he went through wooden chests, trousseaus, wardrobes,

dressers, end tables, and the like. He ended at a shelf of books, sweating now from the heat under the roof and his efforts.

There were many titles that Callum could understand the wisdom in relegating to the attic, but he was confused by a folio of *Twelfth Night* by Shakespeare. It seemed to be handwritten, perhaps from the bard himself! Surely such a treasure would be best kept in a study or library to preserve it.

Callum pulled the folio from the shelf to take it downstairs and show Sam his treasure, when a key and a sealed letter fell from its folds.

"A strange place to keep the key," he murmured to himself, noting the scrollwork on the key matched that on the trunk. He picked the key up, and the letter, and settled himself down on a spindly old chair, which creaked ominously under his weight.

Thinking the letter nothing more than a missive about the folio, perhaps explaining its relegation to the attic, he broke the seal and began to read.

My dearest Samantha,

I am sorry from the bottom of my soul for the burden I have placed upon you.

But I can no longer go on without her.

Take care of your sister.

N

It did not take the clockwork in Callum's brain long to arrive at the conclusion that he'd just unearthed a suicide note.

He hastily secreted it away in his jacket pocket. There was no sense in having one of Sam's old family members unearthed from hallowed ground because he'd stumbled upon a letter proving "N" had committed suicide.

Callum then went to the trunk and unlocked the lid. He pushed it open and saw some rather modern photographs. He then concluded "N" was a fairly recent deceased family member, compared to all the history in the attic.

Sifting through photos and the like, he tried to determine who

"N" was. It didn't take long. In the bottom, left-hand corner of the trunk were a stack of letters, held together with twine. The top one still smelled faintly of perfume.

My dearest Nathaniel,

I am saddened to hear about the loss of your wife. Please know, I will gladly take her place beside you and raise your daughters as my own.

My father is gone, as is yours. My spouse is gone, as is yours. I have no children of my own to worry about. Perhaps now is our time, at last?

With all the love in my heart,

Patricia

Nathaniel Acton, then. An uncle he had not heard Sam or Sabrina mention. And, Callum was certain, his Patricia had died.

He was now entirely entranced by the sad history of Nathaniel Acton. He rustled around in the trunk a bit more, finding hidden mother pictures of two babies and other romantic letters between Nathaniel and Patricia. There was even a wedding portrait of Adelaide and Nathaniel Acton, whom Callum could only assume was Nathaniel's first wife. An arranged marriage, no doubt, since Patricia had been speaking of fathers being gone as though they had been an impediment to their happiness.

Spurred on by this worthy mystery, Callum locked the trunk once more and pocketed the key. He felt the need to pay his respects to Nathaniel Acton, and headed out of the attic and back to his own room to wash his face, shake the dust from his hair, and put on something less grimy.

Callum strode out of the manor house in search of the vicarage, and found it by way of the church, a helpful young man with a cart full of hay pointing him in the right direction. Since there was a graveyard next to the church, he decided he might not need the vicar after all and could just find Nathaniel in the graveyard.

As it turned out, Nathaniel's was one of the newest stones, standing proudly between the headstones of Adelaide and Patricia

Acton. So, the poor man had been allowed his Patricia after all, at least for a short while.

He read the inscriptions on the stones.

Adelaide Acton

Beloved wife of Nathaniel

Mother of Samantha and—

His blood froze.

Mother of Samantha and Sabrina

Hand shaking, Callum traced the letters. S-A-B-R-I-N-A. S-A-M—A-N-T-H-A.

His eyes flicked past Nathaniel's, which necessarily recounted little of how he'd died, to Patricia's.

Patricia Acton

Beloved wife of Nathaniel

Died in a fire.

He stumbled back and ended up flat on his backside on the ground.

SAMANTHA.

SAM—ANTHA.

Callum was stunned. He couldn't move for the longest time.

Then he struggled to his feet and ran back to the house. He passed Anne on the way back to the attic and stared at her a moment.

He could see the realization dawn in her eyes, and he knew that she knew. And he knew that she knew that he knew.

"Your Grace!" Anne called as he pushed past her. "Please, let me explain!"

Callum didn't hear a word. His blood pounding in his ears, he climbed back into the attic and straight back to the trunk, the forgotten folio on the floor next to it. He unlocked the trunk once more and snapped the lid open, digging among the photos.

He turned over one of the hidden mother photos to see writing on the back.

Twins. Samantha and Sabrina Acton

Trembling with emotion, he pocketed the picture, carefully closed and locked the trunk, and picked up the folio.

Twelfth Night. How fitting. Viola would be quite proud.

Callum tucked the folio under his arm and left the attic.

Anne was waiting for him in the hall. "Your Grace, please allow me to speak with you."

Callum shook his head. "You're not the one I want to speak with." He pushed past her and went straight to the sitting room, where he saw Sabrina and Theo sitting on the settee together. It didn't bother him one bit, which should have told him from the beginning he wasn't truly interested in Sabrina.

Not Sabrina.

"Where," he said evenly, "is Sam?"

The lovers stared at him. He could see the wheels turning over in their minds, and knew in an instant that somehow, sometime, Theo had found out the secret. And hadn't told him.

"Tennant." He rose. "What—?"

"Where," Callum growled dangerously this time, "is Sam Acton?"

Sabrina's hand shook slightly, but she pointed. "The study."

"Thank you." His tone was as clipped as his boots on the floor as he made his way to the study.

They had much to discuss, Sam—*antha* and himself.

Found Out

Sam

Sam was just finishing a chapter when the study door slammed open. She jumped, then looked up to see a sweating, read-faced, very, *very* angry Callum in the doorway. He held up a picture with a shaking hand.

"Who," he demanded, "is Samantha Acton?"

She stared at him, not the picture. She didn't need to see the picture. "Would you mind closing the door?"

Callum kicked it shut with his boot so hard it rattled in its frame.

"Thank you." She stood at her desk, as tall as she could, genteel and calm, her arms crossed behind her back. "I'm not sure where you got that."

"I got it where your father left it," he seethed. "And that's not the point. Who is Samantha Acton?"

"She died in a fire when she was five. Poor sister," Sam said, pacing over to look at her bookshelves and not at him.

He backed her up against the shelves, slamming the photo next to her head, surely doing damage to some of the spines of the books he'd hit. And the photo itself. "Don't lie to me," he snarled.

Sam still did not meet his eyes. "It's as much of the truth as you need to know for now."

Callum gripped her chin and forced her to look at him. "You will tell me the whole truth right now, Sam—antha."

"What is there to tell that you don't already know?" she asked bitterly.

He pressed his leg between hers and would certainly ascertain the real truth against his thigh. Or rather, not against his thigh. "Samantha."

"I go by Sam," Sam said. "And am as I have always been. Is that what you wanted to know? Have you satisfied your curiosi—"

Callum gripped her by the throat. "Why would you torture me this way?"

"Torture you? *Torture you?!* You know nothing about torture!" Her eyes narrowed. "I have had to be this-this *thing* for almost all of my life. Not a woman. Not a man. But something in between! What was I supposed to do, hmm? Give Acton to Jeremy? Allow him to make Sabrina miserable in marriage and mistreat the servants and workers on the estate? My father was right in raising me a boy. I was made unmarriageable by fire. *If* I were to marry, how would I explain my situation to a woman? *If* I loved a man..." Sam swallowed and looked at Callum's shoulder rather than his face. "... well, who would want me anyway..."

"I would." Callum's mouth descended, and he ground his lips against hers, forcing her mouth open by pressing down on her chin so he could explore her with his tongue.

She squeaked in mild protest, but then melted against him, the kiss drugging. Her arms found their way up around his neck, and as the kiss went on, she ground against his thigh instinctively.

He dropped the picture and pulled her against him, and Sam could feel the swell of his manhood through both of their trousers. "Fuck it," he hissed, and dragged Sam away from the bookshelves only to sweep the desk clear of everything on it, including the blotter.

"Anne will not thank you for spilling ink all over the—" Sam began, but it ended on a gasp as Callum ripped open her vest and shirt in one strong yank, sending buttons flying everywhere. "J-Just what do you think you're—!"

"You know what I'm doing. Don't pretend you don't. And if you want to stop me, you'd better do it now," he rumbled.

Sam panted, looked at the passion in Callum's eyes, a fire that matched her own, and simply gestured to a drawer. "Letter opener."

"Thank you." He reached into the drawer and pulled out the letter opener, then slit the bandages binding her breasts.

She took a deep breath in, now that the bindings were gone, then moaned when he bent over her to take a nipple between his lips and roll it against his tongue.

Still unable to get enough air, she pulled off her cravat, leaving a great deal of skin and burn exposed. She was trying to care, but couldn't, because Callum was taking off his vest and shirt and throwing them aside along with his own cravat.

"Kick off your shoes," he ordered her.

Sam swallowed and toed off her shoes, one at a time.

Once that was done, he gripped the waistband of her trousers and pulled them off, breeches and all.

She was distantly aware that Callum could now see the full extent of her scarring, except that which was in her shirtsleeve and that which descended beneath her stockings. She bit her lip and tugged at the fabric of her buttonless shirt to pull it over the worst of the scarring, but he batted her hands away and yanked the shirt open even further.

"You have nothing to be ashamed of. You are beautiful, Samantha Acton. Even here." He ran his fingertips over her scars, then followed the path from her ear to her waist with his lips.

Sam's eyes stung with unshed tears. "I-I—"

"You don't need to say anything. Nothing at all." Callum cupped her cheek and kissed her lips again, his anger having turned into a hunger that she didn't know if she could quench.

While they were kissing, Callum fumbled with the front of his trousers. Soon, his manhood sprang free of its cloth prison and she made the mistake of glancing down. Her eyes widened.

"Do you intend to put that thing inside me?! Tennant, it's monstrous!" Sam gasped.

"I assure you, a woman's body is meant to give birth to a whole baby where I'm about to go," he whispered, kissing her again to distract her. "This should not be too much of a challenge. And call me Callum."

"C-Callum," she repeated.

He smiled against her lips. Then his fingers trailed up her thigh and found her most secret place.

Sam nearly bowed off the desk. "Callum!"

"It's okay. I'm just making space," he cooed back, kissing and worshiping her breasts back to life after weeks of being restrained.

What he did with his fingers was truly sinful. Her fingernails dug into the desk as he worked, her body shuddering an orgasm when he was three fingers in.

She was just at the end of her throes of pleasure when he withdrew his fingers and replaced them with something else.

"Deep breaths," Callum said. "You probably still have your impediment and you may feel a sharp pain, but only once." He kissed her, then pushed slowly inside until Sam felt there was, indeed, something stopping him. And it burned when he pressed against it.

"Please tell me it's all inside," she whimpered.

"About half. Give me a moment. Deep breaths," he replied. Then he drew his hips back, then thrust hard.

Sam cried out, her hands, which had moved back to Callum's neck, making grooves on his back.

"It's okay. It's okay. Deep breaths," he said, cradling her. "You'll be fine."

"That's easy for you to say!" she protested, but, indeed, soon the pain faded to a dull ache, especially when he started moving again.

Callum kept kissing and rubbing his hands over her affection-starved body. When he made a low sound in his throat, Sam knew he was reaching his own orgasm.

Though she didn't expect to, she came with him, not as hard as she had around his fingers, but enough to draw another cry from her lips as Callum groaned and spilled his warm seed inside her.

"Is," Sam panted. "Is that all you wanted to discuss?"

He pressed his head against her shoulder for a few moments, then let out a growl. "Not even close," he said, pulling his manhood out of her and flipping her over so she was bent over the desk.

"Callum?" Sam asked, looking over her shoulder at him.

Callum traced his fingers over the burns on her back. "Trust me, Samantha. We are not nearly finished yet."

Also by M. Francis Hastings

Once Bitten

Submitting to My Stepbrother series

Stranded With My Stepbrother

Snatched With My Stepbrother

The Beguiling Baronets series

Deceiving the Duke

Sign up for my newsletter here: https://subscribepage.io/TfsA3A